William Henry Babcock

Cypress beach

William Henry Babcock

Cypress beach

ISBN/EAN: 9783743350076

Manufactured in Europe, USA, Canada, Australia, Japa

Cover: Foto ©Andreas Hilbeck / pixelio.de

Manufactured and distributed by brebook publishing software (www.brebook.com)

William Henry Babcock

Cypress beach

FIRST AMERICAN EDITION.

CYPRESS BEACH

BY

WM. H. BABCOCK.

"A PLACE FOR IDLE EYES AND EARS,
A COBWEBBED NOOK OF DREAMS."

"AND A WIDE WORLD OF WILD REALITY."

"WELL MAY SLEEP PRESENT US FICTIONS,
SINCE OUR WAKING MOMENTS TEEM
WITH SUCH FANCIFUL CONVICTIONS
AS MAKES LIFE ITSELF A DREAM.'

WASHINGTON, D. C.:
WM. H. BABCOCK.
1890.

R. Beresford,
PRINTER,
Washington, D. C.

DEDICATION.

———

To the author of "Elsie Venner" and kindred works, wherein fancy, lightening or darkening but always kindly human, plays very near the depths of mystery and terror; the one living American writer in whom the fascination of the great shadows never has lessened the love of sunshine, nor the willingness, and more than willingness, to shed it abroad. As one who has thriven under it and found enjoyment and profit in all his moods, I feel like quoting, though perhaps with an unwarrantable wrench of the meaning, "Strange is the gift that I owe to you."

PREFACE.

———

Now a preface is a thing of many uses. It may serve to convey a man's ideas of most problems in the universe; but I prefer to reserve the main body of my text for that, and even then there is generally something left over. It may be in itself a delicate and original piece of art in the humorous vein;—if one were only a Nathaniel Hawthorne to make it so. Or it may turn benevolent and save the "chorus of indolent reviewers" all trouble of looking farther.

It certainly did seem to me when once upon a time I set before the public an unpretending structure of verses, that in some way I had made the vestibule too seductive. Most of my newspaper friends who did not devote their energy to contradicting each other were well content to lie down in it, after the fashion of a man coming home very late indeed to a doubtful welcome. Any foot-rug of a quotation from my preliminary prose would serve them for a covering. But this was long ago, and there were things in that poetry which may have merited worse treatment.

However that may be, I wish to have the present story read, a little of it at any rate—and it is not very long—even by the running journalist. It probably will not hurt him; for I know well the capabilities of that tribe, having sinned and suffered in my time, as one of them, although not for long. And "an enduring mind have the destinies appointed to the children of men."

For this present I have in view nothing worse than a brief explanatory chat with my hypothetical readers that are to be. My American readers, for the book, first published in England

to secure that copyright, now comes newly before *them*. Perhaps there may be a dozen copies in libraries and private
hands in this country; and the Government, more or less
wisely, has absorbed and hidden a larger batch beyond all
finding in the labyrinth of the New York Circumlocution
Office. But this is not publication. It is rather keeping the
book a profound and inscrutable secret. And I may safely
assume that you, my dear sir, madam or miss, have never set
eyes on it.

Briefly, then, do not make the mistake of thinking that any
of my characters mean *you*. Something like a year ago this
misadventure befel. I had concocted a very harmless "inter-
ference" yarn, which appeared in Lippincott's magazine for
August, 1889, under the title "An Invention of the Enemy."
It was meant to be satirical, but not unkindly; didactic only
in its undertone and intimations; truthful, and therefore with
plenty of laugh in it. One of the personages did not quite
escape the merry shadow which dogs all of us, understood
rightly. "What fools *we* mortals be." He was upright,
honorable, aspiring, diligent in his calling, exceptional in the
matter of conscience, a reputable man, a good man, a gentleman—only instructively and deprecatedly official. His value
lay in that last foible, more than he could know. In spite of
it he was a friend of mine, this Eben Mumm. As novelists
are given to say, I came to feel rather better acquainted with
him than if he had ever precisely existed in the flesh. I feel
so still.

Now it was very interesting to see how many other gentlemen in office had not the least suspicion in the world that
they could be meant; and felt uneasily compelled to assure
me so. Without exception they were men whom I esteem,
though probably not more perfect than the rest of their gen-
eration. How they and their friends worked out the identity
was now and again a matter of puzzle to me; but generally a
little reflection would throw some light on the process and the
clew.

Now, therefore, I enter my caveat in advance. Let no man find his double in Cypress Beach, for better or worse, for good or ill. The people who stood for my portraits never were born. They died long ago. And they have gone—to Europe. It is the business of a romancer to romance. As to the scenes, you might find some of them ; but others are hardly extant out of dreamland. In particular I do not advise any explorer to undertake the search after the haunted cove, or the ancient village of Nodaway. And now I will end this letter and leave the tale to you.

WM. H. BABCOCK.

ROCK HAVEN, *July 1st, 1890.*

CONTENTS.

CYPRESS BEACH.

CHAPTER I.

ACCOMAC.

In a secluded, rarely-visited, slowly-changing region, where the outposts of a semi-tropical vegetation mingle (as dream-forms mingle) with old English survivals in architecture and human life, a narrow, cypress-shaded river winds its bronze waters down to the great bay. In all our land there is nothing more quaint and winning, more remote and other-worldly. Here again and again has a romantic past made its unavailing stand for royal or feudal shadows, so that the very earth and air are sown with discrowned hopes and foredoomed endeavors.

Hither (now as much a shadow as any) drifted, in the latter days of the merry though baleful King Charles, one who is said to have been in a certain sense very near the throne. Perhaps the exceeding, almost rumor-proof, quiet of her new home may have had its balm for nerves outworn by the glitter and stress of court life, in a time when tragedy and deadly sin went masked as mirth and jeweled bodices hid secrets not lightly to be told.

Yet possibly even in this colonial nook she did not altogether escape the sinister thrill of far-away whispers, such as have left some traces in tradition even to our day. She is always alone, whether shunned or shunning, in the glimpses which this medium gives us; now leaning with stately grace

beside her library window while the sunshine wakes strange
fire in her jeweled fingers; now bowing wistfully over the
spotless white rosebuds of her terraced garden; now pacing
feverishly the narrow strip of sand at the head of the cypress-
bordered cove below.   It is in this latter mood that superstition still loves to picture her in the hush of starlit nights—the
black cypress shadows before and behind, the curved white
beach between, and thereon the phantom of a jeweled lady pacing by the dull-gleaming water—pacing under dread urgence,
with bowed head and hands clasped together! And see, on
one of the bloodless fingers, what is it that glows and changes,
instinct with evil life?

But we need not dwell at present on The Lady of the Ring
or the vagaries of frightened negroes and beclouded loiterers.
Doubtless she made a quiet ending, like many another worn-
out soul, and has been glad enough to remain at rest ever
since, whatever needless tasks may have been assigned her by
a popular ideal of propriety in spectral things, involuntarily
laying emphasis on that one of her belongings which best
typifies her perilous love of the world's brilliancy.

She left by will the ownership of Cypress Beach, with its
mansion of black-glazed English brick and a thousand or more
poorly cultivated, but fairly reliable, acres to a relation (some
said a son by an early marriage) who bore the old Scotch
moss-trooper name of Armstrong.   This vigorous stock, thus
transplanted to new soil, had thriven mightily therein and
never lost its hold.   The estate had alternately expanded and
shrunken many times in the course of political and financial
changes; but there had always been an Armstrong at Cypress
Beach, and he had always been a power in his own neighborhood at least.   The county was pretty well sprinkled with col-
lateral younger scions, which from time to time had dropped
to earth and rooted themselves after the manner of the ban-
yan fig-tree.   They all owned slaves, while slaves were to be
had, and land, unless ill-fortune forbade them to own anything.

One of these servants, a gift from the main family stem at Cypress Beach, was a bright mulatto woman, who became known as Mammy Charlotte with advancing years. In her youth Charlotte had been considered handsome, an endowment, whencesoever derived, which certainly had not been transmitted to the comical piccaninny who was her only offspring. For a time this little John was the plaything of both old and young at Cypress Beach, and the mother received all kindly attention. Then a certain Miss Jessica, niece to Roger Armstrong, the head of the family, came into life at a distant farm; and her baby needs called for the separation of mother and child. Accordingly, with no intention of cruelty, or diminution of good-will, but simply as a matter of supposed necessity, Charlotte was taken from her own infant and sent to care for a child whom she had never seen.

Most slaves would not have found a tragedy in this, and probably Charlotte did not; although, as we shall see, the violation of nature's order had consequences in store for all concerned. Yet, as she bent dutifully over her new charge in the slow hours of the night, how can one doubt that the vision may sometimes have risen before even her of another child whom she might seldom see again, and whose quaint ways would go on amusing and delighting all but her?

But Charlotte's private griefs, if there were such, found no outward expression and gave rise to no ill-will. Before long not even the lady mother was fonder or prouder of little Jessica, and this love of the slave nurse extended in a less degree to the entire household. Therefore, when it was determined that her stay in it should be permanent, she made no strenuous objection; and when misfortune drove her new master to accept a minor official position at Washington, she went with him very willingly and rejoiced in the modest prosperity which followed. Emancipation came, but she remained; and after Jessica's parents had been successively removed by death the old nurse was still at hand to lean on and to trust. Stronger ties than any which could be woven or broken by human law were sure to bind Mammy Charlotte until her last day on earth.

Meanwhile her son John, after having been indulged, was repressed, when repression became necessary, with more harshness than wisdom, so that freedom found him ripe for evil. All the Caliban traits born with him, and fostered by his experience of caprice, showed themselves in a series of crimes, evincing some shrewdness and more brutality. At last, after undergoing divers punishments at the hands of the law, he had disappeared altogether.

Jessica was not a penniless orphan. Her father had recovered something from the wreck of his rural property, and, having but one child and no very expensive habits, had been able to put by more or less money from his salary every year. This process had continued a surprisingly long time considering the political bias of the Armstrongs of Accomac. But he had all the joviality of that well-fed race without much of their aggressiveness; and no one in power cared to molest a man who made himself so pleasant. So Death was the first autocrat who took the matter up with serious hostile intent, and even he considerately waited until Jessica was decently provided for.

But it seemed likely to be a rather meagre support; so, and for other reasons, Jessica accepted after a time an invitation from her widowed uncle Roger to preside over Cypress Beach. Of course Mammy Charlotte went with her; as did also a young gentleman of the capital named Robert Chauncey. Jessica never traveled far without a male escort, partly because it seemed to her rather woman's-rightish and indecorous. She was apt, moreover, to doubt whether such independence were a matter of choice with those who adopted it; and to extend her amiably depreciating pity to women who were less favored than herself by the operation of the great law of demand and supply. There was always a competition among men for her company even on minor occasions.

This would not have seemed strange to any man who looked on Miss Jessica in her twentieth year. She owned a border-state face, a compromise face, yet a very sweet one. Its expression was equally removed from the luxurious fire-veiling languor of the far South, and the nervous energy and keenness of the North; but with hints of both, and now and then a decided lapse toward either. Her form and features were just full enough not to be in the least out of symmetry; her complexion had a soft, human warmth which rarely became quite rosy; and her motions were exceedingly light and graceful. In her manner there were often little turns and ways which some women called "affected," though with no very good reason. Her delicacy of taste was only one form of an extreme susceptibility, that showed itself in some more fantastic if not menacing ways. For example, she sometimes thought she heard her name breathed in low tones when no one was near; and there were certain experiences which might pass for optical illusions, though she did not consider them such. One or two hypnotic experiments, into which unwise companions had led her, were hurriedly given up in sheer indefinable dread of what might follow. She rarely spoke of such experiences; having no desire for the rather unladylike reputation of a seer.

It is beyond doubt that Jessica took a kitten-like pleasure in stimulating the rivalry of her suitors and making life interesting to them by tantalizing bits of caprice; although any suggestion of a serious effort to attract or retain an admirer would have made her open her eyes in disgusted astonishment. In the present instance she had characteristically set aside the man whom she secretly preferred, and accepted as escort one who was only her second choice. Miss Jessica could make second choices with surprising celerity in small matters as well as great. Her present selection was not a bad one.

There was a dash of genius about Robert Chauncey—that is, passive genius, including an exquisite appreciation of the

less obvious beauties of literature and art, but inspiring no
vigorous effort.   He did just enough in several lines to pro-
voke gratifying expostulations for not doing more.   Earnestness of any sort seemed to appal him.   Nevertheless he
nourished a certain half-sentimental sympathy with those
classes which (in that spring and early summer of 1877)
filled the background of every social picture with the shadows of coming revolt.   This had its root partly in a kindly
fellow-feeling for human suffering; but partly, also, in his
own bitter sense of the unequal distribution of wealth.
Sometimes it seemed very hard to him that the luxuries
of life were poured without stint on many who could not
adequately enjoy them, while he had only the meagre indul-
gencies of a department clerk.   He could not help feeling a
longing for some communistic short-cut to (a rather conventional) Utopia; something that would not call for the hopeless virtues of energy, self-denial, and frugality.   His chief
annoyance was a lurking dissatisfaction with himself (perhaps
as yet the only hopeful indication about him), which gave rise
to hazy fancies of proving by some sort of sudden pyrotech-
nics his right to stand forth from the crowd.   But neither
department work nor the routine of fashionable society offers
much scope for exhibitions of that sort, and he saw no present prospect of astonishing anybody.

He was fond of making love of a kind pretty well understood by all parties as predestined to end in nothing.   Most
young ladies of his set were willing to engage in this game,
with a certain sense of being complimented thereby.   It was
perhaps because Jessica Armstrong never showed any reliable
indications of such willingness that he had at last concluded
to consider his affections as seriously engaged, and to conduct
himself accordingly.   At one time he had drawn not a little
hope from the kindly way in which she used her eyes, and
the slightly drooping interest of her attitude: but he generally found his sentimental advances repelled by a wide-awake,
mocking good humor and a truly paralyzing politeness.

Jessica had not passed through two or three Washington seasons and as many episodical engagements for nothing.

Robert Chauncey's campaign against her heart had now been prosecuted for a long time.

He, as well as all other parties concerned, felt that matters were nearing a climax, though the result was past foreseeing. His selection as an escort was hopeful; but, as if measurably to counterbalance it, he knew that she had invited to Cypress Beach his rival who had been left behind, and that the latter had promptly accepted the invitation, even signifying his intention to avail himself of it within two or three days. This rival was a Virginian of considerable attainments and broken fortunes, descended on the mother's side from a noble exiled family of Rochelle through a line of unyielding South Carolina Huguenots, pro-slavery Puritans who hated the anti-slavery Puritans of the North with a holy and a scornful hatred—a man not devoid of sympathies truly, but with a deal of iron in his convictions and his methods of enforcing them, an exalted theory of what was due to himself, and hardly more than an incidental estimate of the value of human life. Chauncey was astonished that Captain Hawksley should have been so complaisant in this instance, after what he must have regarded as a slight put on him. It could only be explained by the eagerness of immediate and very serious intentions.

The trip was a delightful one, both to Jessica and her friend—a sort of merry drama, with much shifting of scenes, to which Mammy Charlottee, with her unobtrusive ways and quiet smile, pleased by her young mistress's pleasure, formed a kindly chorus. It was gay with life when the June sun shone on the sparkling, ruffled waters of the bay; glorious when the sunset's gold lay broken along that liquid floor and vivid cloud-splendors were below as well as above; spiritual in its beauty when the moon swept slowly over heaven, paled now and then by the thin cloud veils that passed her; weird and grotesque in its solemnity, yet with some elements of a fascinating, unearthly grace, as they steamed up the Stygian river between the feathery wading cypresses in the early brightness of another day.

At the landing nearest Cypress Beach they were surprised not to find the old family carriage awaiting them; but a row-boat was moored to the wharf, and Noah, the taciturn negro oarsman, came forward touching his cap. They entered the boat, and were rowed some distance up the river to a point where a brook-like water-way led to a round land-locked cove. Above the opposite shore of this little sheet rose the gardens and walls of Cypress Beach. .

As they sped toward this ancestral home, Jessica let her fingers trail in the water; laughing to herself in a musical, infantine way, which seemed, in the sunshine, to cover her face with bright ripples. One of her mannerisms often de-nounced by women, but somehow liked by most men, was to revert fitfully to the speech and behavior of very early girl-hood. There was no particular forethought about it; and she still looked undeniably too young to seem at all ridiculous.

Glancing up with demure roguishness, she said—

"How I should like to find something that Mr. Chauncey cannot paint!"

Then pointing toward the beach, she cried, with a sudden mock animation of manner—

"There it is! There it is!"

Shaking her head comically, she announced, "No, no, he can't do that." Then, sinking back, she added, "Jessica thinks so," in a complacent, purring sing-song. In her baby moods she was fond of mentioning herself in the third person.

Chauncey answered in a half-playful but significant voice—

"It is very pleasant to be thought about at all by——"

He did not imitate her reference to herself, being stopped by an unmistakable change of manner.

"By *Miss* Jessica Armstrong—is it possible you mean that? O, these men—these men!"

"They *are* a bad lot," he admitted, thoughtfully. "I have always suspected they were a flaw in the scheme of the universe."

"Ah!" exclaimed she, shaking her head with merry knowingness; "you are not to evade my challenge. Now, *could* you paint the secret of that beach with its contrast? Oh, I know you would treat it symbolically; you would give us a grinning African with his teeth all in sight."

He paused in critical doubt. "If our good friend Noah there would only smile his very best."

"What Noah?" she answered, laughing lightly. "Noah never smiles." With that she couched her head sidewise and looked archly at her dark attendant; but his face kept all the decorous blankness of a pall. "Noah smile?" she repeated with an uneasy, quizzical look, "Not he! not if Doomsday were coming to-morrow!"

"Miss Jessie!" murmured Mammy Charlotte, in a frightened, deprecating voice.

"Never mind, Maumee," purred the young mistress, caressingly; "it isn't, you know."

But even while she spoke her eyes followed those of Robert Chauncey to the house above the terraced garden; and she turned away with a shuddering, indrawn breath.

"I cannot look on it," she said, in a low voice. "We are rowing right into a strange mist."

"It is nothing," answered Chauncey, lightly. "An odd play of reflection and the shadow of a cloud going by. Clouds have a right to go by, I suppose? See, it *is* gone."

She looked again. Yes, the old house was in clear sunshine. She could see no cloud in the sky.

CHAPTER II.

"MONARCH OF ALL I SURVEY."

Jessica had hardly landed when a tumult arose beyond the house. A full voice, which might have been heard a mile, roared, "John! Jahn! Jawn! Noah! Sam! Hi-i! Whoo-ee!" Then there was a pause, followed by prodigious emphasis. "You infernal rahscals! Hyaar, John! Zounds and death! John!"

Chauncey looked at his companion in dismay. He could no more have roared at anybody than he could have wrecked a railway train. "Has anything broken loose about here?" he asked.

Jessica laughed merrily. "Only Uncle Roger," she replied. "He is in a hurry for the servants to put away his horse so that he can come and meet us."

"Ah, I see," he replied, dryly; "quite unique and interesting."

"Oh, yes," she replied, roguishly, "and he will find your comment equally so."

Chauncey whistled just above his breath and looked round as if seeking an outlet.

Before he spoke there came plunging down the terraces a bright-eyed, shaggy, grey colt, unbridled and saddleless, with a sunny boy of ten astride of him, who tossed his arms in time with his disordered hair, and called gaily as he rode. Just as this young Bedouin seemed about to wreak destruction upon his guests, he sheered aside, and after one or two curvetings dropped to the ground before them.

"Cousin Jessie, Cousin Jessie!" he cried, in delight. "I'm so glad you've come! 'Deed, 'ndeed I am! We'll have heaps an' heaps of fun now!"

"*That* we will, Prince!" replied Jessica, as she stooped and kissed him, using the nickname which had been earned by a certain lordliness in some of the ways of this little Roger, her uncle's grandson, and an orphan like herself.

Prince broke out again, "I said you'd come! I knew you'd come! Gran' would have it you wouldn't be here till to-morrow, but he don't know you like *I* do, Cousin Jessie. I *made* Noah go after you."

Then he seemed to become aware that he was ignoring her escort, and turned to the latter with a shy, native courtesy that sat rather stiffly on him as yet.

"I beg pardon, sir," he said; "I am right glad to see you. But I only saw——" and he turned toward Jessica with a light laugh, as though the sight of her melted all his little ceremony.

Robert Chauncey's heart warmed toward this small gentleman who had blundered instinctively on so high a compliment.

"Mr. Chauncey," said Jessica, "this is my cousin Prince, sometimes called Roger, this little flatterer."

"Flatterer, Cousin Jessie!" he expostulated, with reproachful dignity; then added, "I am very happy to know you, Mr. Chauncey."

"I can see already that the pleasure will be mutual," responded the latter, with all decorum.

"Won't you walk up?" suggested Prince, turning to lead the way. "Grandfather will be here presently; I heard him at the stables just now. Ah, here's my hat; it blew off as I rode."

"Rode!" exclaimed Chauncey, "I should think you did, my boy! General Putnam might have taken lessons from you."

"General Putnam?" queried Prince.   "Oh, he was a Yankee."   Then, in dread lest he had given offence, he hurriedly added, "But I hope you're not a Yankee."

"Not exactly," answered Chauncey, willing to help him out, "only a New Yorker."

Prince looked puzzled.   All Northerners were Yankees to him, and the term was opprobrious.   But he understood that Robert was not offended, and he felt vastly relieved.

As they neared the house its owner came rolling through the doorway with a sailor-like gait, which yet carried him rapidly, for his abundant adipose was dominated by more abundant muscle.   His large head, which often bent a little forward to keep the bodily balance, was now raised to greet them, showing a broad, high forehead and Jove-like benignity of countenance.   His face seemed the natural abode of sunshine.   All its smiles began in and about his joyous, boy-like, blue eyes, but even his luxuriant brown beard could not effectually hide their spreading.   It was a face susceptible of frowns, too—sudden, brief, and dark as a July storm, and charged with as trenchant lightning.   He would have no compromise with anything that savored of deception or even sordidness.   The hand of the bribe-taker or wire-puller, the tongue of the liar, the heart of the coward, were members which he longed to tear out and trample under foot; and he did so as far as words could effect it.   This terrific and unflinching frankness had almost wrought his exclusion from politics, in spite of his fluency and cogency of speech, his intensity of conviction, his great though often impracticable intellect, and his local influence as the head of a long-respected and many-acred family—a sort of surviving colonial magnate.

Every one felt the charm of his presence and character. The negroes whom he roared at in his fits of impatience had long ago set them down to "his way," knowing that he would never inquire how they voted, nor punish even the most insolent contradiction if they could show truth or justice on their side. The young girls liked him for his patriarchal gallantry; men and women of equal years, for his frank courtesy and constant good spirits; the aged, for his almost reverential regard; but most of all was he worshipped by the rough, gnarled men of the waste places, and by the little children of both rich and poor.

"Why, Jessie!" he exclaimed, radiantly, holding out two rather chubby hands, where the brown freckles almost hid the natural fairness of the fine skin. "Why, Jessie, my darling!" And he bent down to kiss her fresh young face, murmuring in pleased surprise, "Well, well, well! But indeed I did not expect you to-day."

"You didn't, uncle! Why what do we live in this age of wires and lightning for? I certainly made use of them. That is Mr. Chauncey—*pardonnez*, Mr. Armstrong, Mr. Chauncey."

As they shook hands her uncle suggested, "I see some ladies still remember how to keep the youngsters about them. Well, I am glad of it—being the gainer in this instance."

Before Chauncey could bring his compliment to bear, Jessica struck in with a knowing smile and shake of the head—

"Ah, ah! all very well! But, Uncle Roger, if you knew—— Oh, but I *will* tell him, though. Uncle Roger, he wanted to know if 'anything had broken loose.' I think he had suspicions of a menagerie."

Mr. Armstrong looked puzzled for a moment, then began laughing gently. "Oh, it was when I was calling for the men to put away my horse. Well, I *am* a menagerie sometimes. I have some of the slowest niggers on earth. Have to rare on 'em now and then. Can't help it. Well meaning darkeys, too. Confound 'em."

"Anybody would shout to get into Miss Jessica's company," quoth Robert Chauncey. "Even our colored, camp-meeting friends shout to get to heaven."

"That ought to commend you to her good graces," responded the elder man, still laughing. "But they delight in experimenting on our susceptibilities. I say 'our,' for *I* am a boy, too. When the youthfulness goes out of me, I hope the vital spark will not linger. But about the message—I suppose it is pigeon-holed in Nodaway, as usual. I regret exceedingly that I did not receive the intelligence in time to have the carriage at the wharf. But come, I musn't leave you in the sun and the outer atmosphere. Jessie, you are lady of the house now. An old widower's establishment, Mr. Chauncey; pray make allowances."

It was characteristic of Roger Armstrong, that he rarely mentioned the air as such. He could use the simplest and most direct Saxon on occasion; but latinized English was his normal vehicle of thought and speech. Sometimes this had a quaint effect. A bit of fresh human feeling wrapped in these polysyllabics seemed very like a rosy-faced darling masquerading in the state dress of her grandmother.

As Chauncey and Jessica passed on before him, Mr. Armstrong felt Prince tugging at his coat, and turned to hear the query—

"Gran, what did he mean when he said he was a New Yorker, but not a Yankee?"

The grandfather looked alarmed. "My boy," he exclaimed, in the lowest tone his voice would take; "I hope you have not been indulging in any unwise allusions. Remember that a gentleman never says anything to wound the feelings of another. I know of no surer test."

"I didn't mean to," replied the boy, with quivering lips.

Roger Armstrong beamed down upon him and patted his sunny hair, saying, "I am sure of it."

After dinner—the old-fashioned noonday meal—he took Robert Chauncey out for a visit to the stables, a drive, and a general inspection of the farms. It was a purely conventional proceeding on both sides. Chauncey could not possibly have declined any invitation from a host, and the elder gentleman was dominated by a dreadful sense of propriety which forbade him to omit the customary attention to a guest. So, though the one longed to remain about the house (where Jessica was), and the other must, at least, have suspected his longing, and both of them would have preferred to gratify it, they combined to remove him to very different scenes.

Robert Chauncey, however, had a humming-bird's easy consolability, and his artist's eye turned with something more than a good grace to the perfectly formed barb, plunging and curveting in a circle at the end of his tether, around the warily-turning, proud-faced groom. But when he heard an abnormally fat hog commended as "beautiful," and was informed that the true test of a sheep's beauty was its "approximation to the form of a parallelogram," he began most unjustly to suspect an intention to quiz. If Mr. Armstrong could have made a fortune by raising symmetrical animals of the edible species, he would still have gone on fattening them into monstrosities. His triumph in their approach to his ideals would have compensated for any loss.

Mr. Armstrong's farming commended itself to Robert Chauncey, for it was mainly carried on in a buggy. Once or twice a day he drove from farm to farm, and from field to field, consulting and joking with the overseers, inspecting the work of every hand, storming at the lazy or careless, rebuking the cruel, listening to the complaints of the captious, instructing the ignorant or clumsy, encouraging the diligent, and stimulating all. But it may be doubted whether his stentorian censures and exhortations always produced their due effect. The darkey ordinarily scratched his head when his employer's back was turned, with a comical look that foreboded a return to his derelictions.

That evening Chauncey was made aware of some other peculiarities of his host. The latter, who was in fine spirits and desirous of entertaining, soon took the conversation entirely to himself, and narrated story after story with infinite action and no little imitative power. Chauncey did not know (and Mr. Armstrong himself certainly did not,) how many times these anecdotes had done duty before. They made up all in all a standing stock of about forty, which

almost seemed to have been labeled and set aside for future
reference.   Three or four related to his early college life;
every trip that he had made to the great cities of the North,
had added another; electoral and legislative experiences had
thrown in a small quota; something had been derived from
the efforts of negroes to escape in the old patrol days, and
from the stormier experiences of the war; and the great bulk
of the remainder were derived from his observation of strange
characters and incidents in his immediate neighborhood.
Taken down as he told them, they would have made a very
instructive and racy panorama of a vanished or vanishing
order of things.

In repeating these the old gentleman showed as great
delight as his auditor; but when the latter attempted a story
of his own (presuming on an established city reputation for
quaintness and vivacity of humor and the power of placing
salient points in a novel light,) Roger Armstrong's eyes began
to blink before the third sentence was uttered.   Chauncey
hurried on to the thrilling climax, but just before it was
reached he saw a series of nods end in a dead sleep.   Then
Jessica, who had been unusually still, came to his aid with an
offer to play something.   As they moved toward the piano,
they heard her uncle's sudden voice—"Exceedingly interesting, sir, exceedingly interesting!"

Then he nodded off again, while Jessica, smiling sedately,
touched the keys.   The smile died away as her fingers and
soul seemed to flow in accord from note to note of the unearthly music which she had chosen, the Spirit Waltz of
Beethoven.   Her rendering of this had always a special
quality, but now its effect was so subtly heightened that
Chauncey found himself wondering what could have happened during his absence.

CHAPTER III.

Something *had* happened. On finding herself left queen regnant, Jessica naturally undertook a sort of general visitation of her indoor realm; the rather disorderly kitchen with its broad-faced, grinning occupant, the cellar-dairy with its row on row of creaming milk-pans and its half-dozen barrels of well-ripened peach brandy, the parlor, the dining-room, and the sleeping apartments, all in their diverse bravery of old-time furniture and ornament. There was doubtless much that might have been changed for the better; but she found a pleasure in noting that no iconoclastic reforms had been in progress since her last visit.

Before she had quite satisfied her mind on this point, Prince pounced upon her and carried her off with familiar turbulence for a "pull on the cove." While this proud young oarsman sent their boat dexterously in and out of the cypress shadows, a curious thought mounted from her heart to her lips.

"Prince," asked she, suddenly, "what is there behind the great panel above the dining-room fireplace? It stands out *so* much at one end"—indicating with her fingers the size of the gap.

"No, Cousin Jessie, not that much," protested the boy. 'I flung a ball against it last winter and loosened it."

"But what is in there? What did you find?" she asked.

"Oh, nothing," he answered; "'deed that was all. I only peeped in a little. I reckon there's only a big hole, a great

3   17

square, empty place, like there is behind all the panels over the mantelpieces. They sound hollow when you hit 'em."

"So there was nothing," persisted she, musing.

"Dead loads of it; and I saved the whole treasure against your coming, Miss Curiosity," he replied, pertly.

She menaced him with uplifted hand, but he did not look alarmed.

"Prince," asked she again, presently, "will you help me to look behind that panel when we get back?"

"That I will," he answered, with a look of surprise. "But can't we let the panel alone for a little while? We can get to see what there is behind it easy enough by and by."

"Oh, yes," she responded, lightly, and gave herself to the frolic with such zest that the afternoon was far spent before they returned to the house.

Mounted on chairs before the loosened panel, the two pryed away in diligent expectation; till suddenly it fell outward with a crash, and a great cloud of soot and mould and plaster. Jessica, uttering a little shriek, sprang aside just in time to avoid the shower; but her cousin, according to the luckless doom of boys, was less fortunate. A sharp outcry, which even his ambition of manhood could not suppress, showed that for the moment he was blinded. Hence he did not see the fall of a thick roll of charred paper, nor the quick motion of his companion, who seized and secreted it, as she hurried to his assistance. She acted on impulse in this; and afterward refrained—she hardly knew why—from mentioning her prize to any one, till night should give her full leisure to examine it.

Before going upstairs that evening, she bent over her dozing uncle and kissed his great forehead. "Assuredly, assuredly!" he exclaimed, looking up quickly.

She laughed lightly, "Assuredly what, dear uncle?"

"Why, why—here it is," fumbling in his waistcoat pocket. "Were you not making inquiry relative to the ring?"

"Ring! What ring?"

"I must have been dozing mighty soundly," he answered, with a good-humored laugh. "I certainly thought you had come, my dear, to upbraid me for my dilatoriness in transferring the ring to your possession. Ah, here it is; your cousin Sarah brought it yesterday for you. It had been mislaid, or put away and forgotten for many years; but she thinks, and I believe correctly, that it can be no other than The Lady's Ring, which, you know, tradition connects with the first occupant of this house. There were at one time all manner of fanciful legends about it, mostly forgotten now I believe, so that it is a very appropriate as well as an unique present for our mystery-loving young lady. Allow me"—and without more ado he slipped it on her finger.

"Am I so very mysterious, uncle?" asked Jessica, in an uncomfortable voice that tried to be mirthful, but without daring to give offence by a superstitious refusal. Nevertheless, something, perhaps the rather ghostly idea of its antiquity and long disuse, sent a cold thrill through her arm and body. She did not, however, allow this to prevent her from going into lady-like raptures over the ring.

"What is it?" she asked, turning the broad face of its single gem toward Robert Chauncey.

"I should call it an opal," he answered. "But no, I have never seen anything just like it. How it changes! Almost as if it were alive! Yes, it is strangely beautiful." He added in an underbreath his usual expletive comment, but with more meaning than the words generally carried—"That is no good thing."

Five minutes later, Jessica, half disrobed and comfortably tumbled into a huge rocking chair, was reading her captured manuscript by lamplight. It was in a lady's hand of bygone days, and must once have been neat as well as clearly legible; but fire had burned away or badly charred many of the pages. As Jessica puzzled over the quaint archaisms and the blurs and blotches that too often obscured the meaning, the fancy grew on her that the writer had tossed the narrative on the nearly dead embers some midnight centuries before, and then, the fire failing to wholly do its work, had hastily snatched up the leaves and crowded them out of sight—as she supposed for ever. There was something very chill and shadow-like in sitting there amid just such another hush of night and reading the secret records of the long dead. The light touch of willow branches on the window panes made her shrink as though a spectral hand warned her back from an unholy task. The low moans of the rising wind as it swept around the old walls seemed instinct with more than elemental complainings. The very chirp of the house-cricket startled her. But curiosity and somewhat more held her to the task.

"I would not be conceived," began the writer, "either peevishly or presumptuously to kick against the decrees of Heaven I hope that I have made that right Christian use of my afflictions: though, in truth, not merited by any pravity of conduct industriously entertained by me or radicated in my nature.

"Well, and with right good conscience, may I call my father notorious, for though His Majesty had withdrawn his countenance from him, yet none the sooner did he receive advertisements by express message that His Majesty was sorely straitened, than he made several cavalcades through the north country for His Majesty's recruit, and did infest in especial those places which displayed a violent affection for the enemy, until that party was reduced to a lowness in those parts, and he did often have good execution upon them. He did apparently, and beyond all question, win the most notable triumphs."

Here followed a number of illegible pages, probably relating to the progress and termination of the civil wars and the restoration of King Charles II. Then came a clear paragraph:

"He had at this time a design presently to marry me; to which purpose he had an overture from a noble family on the behalf of a well-bred, hopeful, young gentleman, who had the honor to be a menial servant to the king in a place near his person."

Then succeeded indistinct reminiscences of court life. Somewhat plainer than the rest were a few words referring to the influence of the monarch over the fair sex. "And they did say that he had a ring, the which was given him by one of the many outlandish women who do company with sturdy beggars from foreign parts. And many there were who questioned whether any woman who wore that gaud could"—the rest of the page was burnt.

A little further on was a longer decipherable passage. "It fell out, as I was but exercising myself one day in the park, that His Majesty, companied by the two dogs that kept with his lesser peregrinations, did of a sudden unthought-fully come out of a by-way; whereat my Spanish jennet, even like any vulgarly spirited creature, did rear in exceeding great panic fear and cast me off on the ground. Surely I should have suffered exceeding from this disgrace, but that the king did with the most industrious promptness retrieve me from all danger, grieving and ·lamenting my dire strait. In sooth, finding myself not likely to suffer nor shrewdly hurt, I could not but be sensible of a delight in His Majesty's solicitude; for he had a very flowing courtesy and such a volubility of manner as surprised and delighted. Nor let it be doubted [*i. e.*, *suspected*] that I set these things down in order in pure gaiety [*i. e.*, *idleness*], for in truth they had serious concernment with my troubles thereafter; wherefore even at this writing I am exceeding grieved and heartless—a sore burden not to be admired at by any who know my story. Yet that day I could see but the pleasantness of his apparent royal favor; the which was the more palpable and notorious, inasmuch as after divers passages of gracious condescension, he would not suffer me to refuse a certain ring of most signal and unique beauty; and charged me straitly to wear the same at all times, in his remembrance. Whereat, I quickly did find myself most notable and of respect in every one's mouth; until——"

The latter part of the narrative was nearly obliterated. Jessica found many indications of external luxury and internal conflict, with frequent allusions to an influence which could not be shaken off. The ring here and there seemed to be an object of aversion and fear, yet the writer had not dared to remove it lest the king should be displeased; and before long all such rebellious desires seemed to have ceased, and the gem was lost to sight in the multitude of adornments lavished upon her. At last something had brought about her sudden downfall and exile; but the final pages which would probably have given the particulars were missing.

Jessica laid aside the charred manuscript, and sat piecing together the hints which it gave, till there rose clearly before her the vision of the proud, lovely woman, gay with her own love of the world's brightness, yielding slowly to the spell which she dared not or could not cast from her, and lured onward by praise and power to—the long heartbreak of this lonesome, colonial nook. To Jessica's society-loving nature even the minor accessories of the catastrophe were tragical.

As she sat thinking, thinking, she seemed to hear close to her ear the one word "Beware!"—very low, almost a whisper indeed, but quite distinct. It was not the first time that her super-sensibility had caused such illusions; but now there was something so sinister and chill in the tone that she looked again and again with a real dread at the mirror in front of her. As she glanced aside at the manuscript the same word stared at her from the charred fragments of the very last page. Bending, shiveringly, she had just made out, as she thought, the further word "ring," when an unlucky movement crumbled the whole passage into soot. She flung the roll from her, and looked in disgust at her soiled fingers. This brought the ring prominently into view (by that light it was of a dull, smouldering red), and her finger, swollen by the day's heat and exercise and the recent pressure of her head upon her hand, seemed to burn under it. She tried impulsively to work off this painful acquisition, but it would not move. The resistance gave her time to ask herself what excuse she could make for its absence to her uncle and the donor. The thought of failing in courtesy or appreciativeness was distressing, especially on account of a fancy-born terror such as she would be ashamed to own. So, laughing to reassure herself, she finished undressing, and "lay down in her loveliness," with the ring still on her finger.

Nevertheless, lying there nervous and wakeful, she found it a sore trial. The sensation of burning persisted beyond all reason, and she fancied that she could see the gem flash with the lightning, and gleam with the flickering of the lamplight, as some adventurous gust shook the windows and blew in through the crevices. She had not been willing to trust herself to the dark, but she had failed signally to bring about anything that could fairly be called brightness. The muffled tumult of the storm, the irregular shadow dance on the thick walls, the eerie noises common at quiet times to wind-visited old houses, all entered into conspiracy with her own inner weakness and startling fancies. A mysterious foreboding and terror weighed on her heart, and she passed from wakefulness to troubled sleep, and from sleep to wakefulness again without any sense of relief. The morning found her pale and worn.

CHAPTER IV.

"HARMONY NOT UNDERSTOOD."

Robert Chauncey was awakened early the next morning by the prodigious voice of his host calling to the overseer's house or to the negro quarter. Then a door opened, and a heavy tramp came down the hall. Roger Armstrong was about to do his letter-writing for the day. His mail was usually a large one, coming from all quarters and dealing with all sorts of subjects. Amateur farmers wished his opinion of hogs or fertilizers, legislative aspirants and office-seekers solicited his influence, commission merchants in the cities held forth on their special facilities, inventors and manufacturers trumpeted their machinery, philanthropists and county-improvers called upon him for aid, friends sent him news of the latest political movements. He felt obliged to answer each of these politely (which generally meant rather voluminously), and the still hours about sunrise had long suited this purpose best.

When Jessica entered the breakfast room her uncle came cheerily forward with his, "How do you come on?" and a cordial kiss, hardly stopping for an answer before greeting Chauncey, and passing thence to the practical business of the occasion. He was too thorough an optimist to suspect any ailment which was not, so to speak, driven into his notice. Beside, it would have seemed to him quite abnormal that an Armstrong should be ill at ease in her ancestral home. She was making a determined effort to seem as though her nerves were not unstrung and her brain hot and weary.

The meal was literally a light breaking of fast on various kinds of bread, with coffee and relishes, but the tendency to chat made it longer than in busier regions.

Prince, spoiled lad that he was, had come to the table considerably after the others. His grandfather accosted him—

"By Zines, boy, but this won't do. Where have you been, sir?"

Prince flushed, but answered straight to the mark—

"I have been riding the bay colt, sir."

"Which I positively prohibited you from mounting," responded the elder Roger, looking like a thunder-cloud. "And thumping him, too, I warrant, by Zines, sir."

Prince looked distressed.

"I hope not, sir."

"Well, sir, you may go to your room and remain there till noon. Promise me that, sir."

Prince, ready to cry with mortification, simply answered, "Yes, sir," and marched to the door.

Jessica refrained from saying, "Poor little fellow!" knowing that pity would be the unbearable last drop in his cup of bitterness.

Robert Chauncey, who could never wholly ignore the humorous side of things, remarked in an undertone—

"It seems that the 'little hatchet' game is not always a success."

When too late he saw that he had been overheard, for Prince tossed his vanishing head in angry scorn, and Mr. Armstrong answered severely—

"There was no 'game' in the case, sir. I trust when my grandson sinks so low as to require an incentive to tell the whole truth, that the providence of God may speedily remove us both, sir."

Jessica saw that there was danger of some unpleasant passages, and exerted herself valiantly to effect a diversion. Luckily neither of the men were given to cherishing grudges, so before the young lady's vivacious story had ended, both were laughing heartily.

"Come," ejaculated her uncle, "it's too bad that the youngster should lose all this. Susan, go up to Mr. Roger's room, and inform him that we desire him to return to his breakfast, d'ye hear?"

It had been said that Smiling Susan would certainly grin at her own funeral. Giggles were respectfully suppressed in the presence of her superiors; but no power on earth could prevent her great cheeks from rippling as they shone, even then. She never had smiled harder than when she thought her employer and his visitor were about to quarrel; and now that she was going on an errand which pleased her mightily, she smiled still.

As Prince re-entered, evidently "in charity with all mankind," his grandfather reached him the hand of welcome, and Jessica (holding herself, however, quite matronly, as not inciting to disorder) encouraged him with—

"We'll find fun enough before school opens."

"Yes, Cousin Jessie;" then, ruefully, "It'll come soon enough;" and then, with a sudden dash of resentment, "and they're going to try to crowd a nig in, too."

"Zounds and death!" exclaimed Mr. Armstrong, "I shall express to the principal of that institution my most unqualified condemnation." His manner added that this would be a dire calamity to that instructor.

Chauncey asked demurely—

"Is he *very* black?"

"No, 'ndeed," answered Prince. "Dirty-yellow-white, mighty near chalk-white, a long way whiter'n *that*"—holding up his sunburnt paw. "But a nigger's a nigger. And if they crowd him in there, he'll get killed."

"Oh! oh!" remonstrated Robert. "That would be no good racket."

"It would be perfectly justifiable," burst out the elder Armstrong, in full blast; "I would do it myself. It is an intuitive impulse implanted in the human heart, sir. Yet I don't blame the poor negro, sir; I blame the devils who will persist in thrusting him where he does not want to go, to make trouble. And as for miserable rahscals like that Ishmael Vamper, who are deluding the ignorant creatures by their vile demagoguery: I could shoot them—I would shoot *him* as I would any other——."

He was interrupted by the hurried entrance of a servant with a letter.

"I hope you will excuse me, Mr. Chauncey," said the Accomac. gentleman, with a marvellous change of tone; " this seems to require instant attention," and he was deep in its contents the next moment. This was not of a character to keep, but may bear transcribing.

" Hell's broken loose in Nodaway. That firebrand, Vamper, is in a fair way to burn us all up. He made a crazy agrarian speech to a crowd of negroes last night, advising them not to work for their former masters, but to band together and raise wages higher and higher to compel a final division of the land. He called upon them to sustain 'the cause of the working men,' and prophesied a general uprising, with all manner of prizes in the way of communism and revenge. This stirred the people, and they have been straggling in ever since daybreak. Thus far there are no injuries except one darkey (pistol-ball in calf of leg); but there have been several affrays, and we may have hot work at any moment. To make matters worse, they say the Wildcatters are coming down in force to lynch Vamper. Now do make haste, dear General"—the country people generally gave him this title, though he had never borne a commission—" and use your influence—no one else has so much—to allay the excitement of the people, and prevent what all must finally regret."

Before the signature was reached, Roger Armstrong had forgotten all his truculence. His only thought now was the necessity of immediate action to avert dire trouble and crime. Without the least consciousness of inward change, and believing himself as ever the most consistent of men, he was about to peril his life as a matter of course to prevent the very deed which he had just announced his readiness to commit in per-

son.   No man understood better than he the lights and shadows
of those unkempt, ague-toughened, Vendean-like foresters—
their wayward generosity, their crude hospitality, their deference for hereditary leaders, their intense religious convictions,
their furious and enduring pugnacity, their occasional unrelenting and frightful cruelty.   Even their best friend would
find little safety between them and their prey.

There was no fear, in his case; but there were certain obsta-
cles which nearly answered the same purpose.   Just as he
reached the door, he remembered that he was neglecting one
of his notable rules of etiquette, which forbade him to leave a
written message without a written answer.   So he turned back
and indited some ten polysyllabic sentences expressing his
great concern at the "calamitous concurrence of circumstances," and his determination to discharge the full measure
of duties "devolving upon every good citizen when his influence may be of service in preventing so deplorable a catastrophe."   This dispatched by the servant who had brought the
letter from Nodaway, he hurried to his "conveyance."

There Jessica awaited him, pale, but without a word to dis-
suade from his main purpose.   She only asked—

"Why *will* you take that balky black?   Shall I tell John to
get another horse?"

"No!   No!" he answered, laughing and kissing her.   After
climbing heavily into his seat, he turned and added: "I am
resolved to break this fellow of his tricks.   His action is won-
derful.   Make my excuses and compliments to Mr. Chauncey,
and assure him that I regret the loss of his society as well as
my breakfast."   Then he drove off.

At no great distance he came on a number of his ewes which
had strayed into the highway, and which one or two of his
"labor" were endeavoring to drive through a gate.   The bewildered creatures moved at cross-purposes or huddled in
seeming obstinacy, blocking the road.   He might have urged
his horse through and scattered them easily enough; but he
never once thought of such an irregular proceeding.   With
him property always dominated the man rather than the man

the property; and farming tradition and routine took precedence of everything except King Death.

The next cause of delay was æsthetic. A fast trotter with excellent "points" and free, noble "action" passed him, and he could not resist the temptation to call the groom back and ask many intricate genealogical questions. After the equine family tree had been exhaustively explored, the horse was put through his paces and duly admired and criticised. Then Roger Armstrong drove on in meditative enjoyment.

But not for long. The splendid black which drew him, having grown properly disgusted with these successive halts, retorted in kind by anchoring himself without orders, an old trick which he was supposed to have outgrown. Armstrong, at last awakening to the lapse of time and the urgency of the crisis, groaned in spirit and grew all afire with impatience Still, he kept a serene face and used only dulcet and persuasive tones. Roaring might do with negroes, but it had no part in his management of horses; and the whip was a discarded and reprobated article. However, his diplomacy elicited no response except a twitching of the ears, which then settled back determinedly. Roger recognized the defiance, and raved away below his breath, before calling sweet names again, and politely requesting him to move on. Next, this strategic driver worked gently on the reins and tried to back, knowing that motion is more easily converted into motion than quiescence is; but the knowing brute turned sufficiently to look one wheel and thereafter held his neck as rigidly awry as if cast in bronze. Some gentle ticklings only made him move his legs as though preparing to launch out against the dashboard. Mr. Armstrong then lowered himself cumbrously to the ground and led his horse. But this grew wearisome to exhaustion, and as soon as he regained his seat the balking began again. He was at his wits' end; and, to make matters worse, the village was now so near that he could hear a most alarming hubbub, broken by reports of firearms. It was a study for a sculptor—the portly, serene, tormented master, and the firmly-planted brute.

CHAPTER V.

"LET LOOSE FOR A SEASON."

Doubtless Ishmael Vamper had once possessed parents and other definite antecedents like other people; but no one seemed to know anything about them. He had brought out of the shadows of his earlier life a kind of intermittent hovering gentility, which prevented him from seeming merely brutal by suggesting something worse. Had there been any substantial good in him, he might have made a notable figure in the world, for he was abundantly supplied with brains, and intense though fitful energy, and that inestimable man-enthralling power which in politics we term "magnetism." Even genius, or rather an uncanny eidolon or semblance of genius, seemed to haunt his soul and flutter about much that he did, like the tenants of Lord Lytton's haunted house—not spirits of the living or the dead, but more frightful counterfeits, without sympathy, purpose, or any human attribute!

After a varied career not profitable to trace, he had found himself in Washington reduced to shabby straits and unkempt disorder. It then occurred to him to turn his very savagery to account at the expense of the legislators of the country. He knew how sensitive a political barometer the ordinary congressman is, and he saw that in such quarters there was a growing terror of what was known as the labor movement, and the discontent and turbulence which were rife everywhere. He set up forthwith as an organizer and agitator, and soon acquired some notoriety and influence. Then he entered on his programme of extortion.

When the card-summoned congressional victim emerged into the hall or the lobby, he would find himself confronted by a sinewy, threadbare, jauntily obtrusive form, a colorless face, mobile yet hard and jeering, and a pair of grey eyes with an unsteady, rather wild light in them : and he would be greeted sardonically in this wise—

"You see before you a son of the people. Unfortunate, sir—poor, but proud! He must be provided for."

Every attempt at evasion was pooh-poohed; every pretence of conscientiousness scourged with truculent sarcasm ; every symptom of coming denial met with the regretful inquiry—"*Must* I then play Lucifer among your constituents?" He would add meditatively, "I *like* to play Lucifer." After some minor successes, chance had led him to train his batteries on the Honorable Frederick De Lancey, whose conservative district had not changed its vote in twenty years. Though rarely opening his chiselled lips in the House, this legislator when at home lived in some state, was generally mentioned as "a man of distinguished appearance," and was regarded as a very great personage indeed. He devoted, justifiably, a considerable part of his leisure time to the work of respecting himself; and he felt that the world was indeed going to the bad when he heard this insufferable fellow make a mock of his provincial glories, and threaten the sacrilege of turning his constituents (*his* constituents!) against him. As soon as he had recovered breath and power of motion, he beckoned to the nearest messenger and handed him a half-dollar. "John," he said, "have the goodness to hear as my substitute whatever this person may wish to say;" and he walked placidly back through the door up the aisle to his seat.

The negro, fully alive to the humor of the situation, straightened himself like a grenadier, and said: "Well, sah, please proceed, ef you please," in a condescending tone, which drew sounds of merriment from the gathering spectators. Vamper cast one venomous look at him, and hurried away pursued by their suppressed laughter and the louder "Yah!

yah! yah!" of the sable proxy.   The latter had a true place-
man's aversion for the displacemen and their leaders.   Moreover, he felt jolly over his easily earned half-dollar.

Ishmael did not disguise to himself that this was a serious
blow.   He knew that the story would spread, and lead to recalcitrancy and ridicule.   He was sorry the issue had been
made in such a Gibraltar of a district; but he felt that now
or never was the time to prove that there was substance in
his threats.   So, collecting what money he could, he departed
ostentatiously, to "organize the working-men," that is, to introduce communistic doctrines and foment discord on the
Eastern Shore.

His past experience as a "carpet-bagger" in the Southern
States misled him.   All his successes had been gained through
the negroes (where they were in a majority), and so he now
addressed himself mainly to that race.   His incisive and vivid,
though rather infernal, oratory was in startling contrast to
the voluminous rhetoric of their former masters, and the
clumsy imitations of their own local leaders: so his fame
widened rapidly.   Portentous crowds flocked to hear him,
work was neglected, and a sense of ill-usage and antagonism
spread abroad.   Offers were not wanting to seize the axe and
the torch when they should receive the promised summons
to join the great uprising.   His reckless invective became
more and more extravagant as he found that nothing was too
wild for his ignorant and excited hearers.   The wrath of both
races was brewing a storm.

While Roger Armstrong was dallying along the road, an
assemblage of negroes in front of the village hotel were
clamoring for another speech from Vamper; and a lesser
party of white townspeople and young farmers, heated by the
quarrels of the last two or three hours, had elbowed their
way into the throng hooting derisively.   No sooner had the
orator appeared on the balcony than a squabble arose below,
and a pistol shot was fired, perhaps by accident or at random;
but it sprinkled him with broken glass from a window at his

side, causing a precipitate retreat. As he listened, seated within, to his dupes, now fighting, running, groaning, outside, he reflected that he had been a fool, and would like very much to get out of the scrape. Then he bolted and barricaded the door, cocked his revolver, and sat quietly down out of line with the window. The struggle in the street was quite over by this time, the negroes having speedily scattered. For the moment, pursuers and pursued had left the field of battle. All was silent except the moans of two or three dark, recumbent figures, which could not conveniently leave the side walk. Then a voice announced significantly: "The Wildcatters," and there was a general return of the whites.

At that cry, Ishmael Vamper leaned sidewise, and looked cautiously out. Directly toward him, entering the village by a side street, came a score or so of gaunt horsemen, two by two, with shot guns on their shoulders, and their faces shadowed by tattered hats of felt or straw. The leading file consisted of a little swarthy, wiry fellow, with a bead-like gypsy eye, and an iron-sinewed, round-shouldered, bony giant of at least six feet three. They rode deliberately, like men who had come on serious business. As they entered the main street, they pointed out the wounded negroes to one another with a word and a scowl, and exchanged rough greetings with friends in the crowd. Then three or four of the party, as though by preconcerted arrangement, kept on to the rear of the hotel, while the main body dismounted and advanced toward the front steps. Vamper breathed hard and set his teeth.

Just then there was a great rushing and clattering down a side street, and Roger Armstrong came hurrying, buggy and all, round the corner. At the last available moment his horse had condescended to go—with the full impetus of a stream bursting its dam. The utmost strength of its owner's powerful arms barely effected a halt a little beyond the hotel steps. Then, with no apology to those who were still tumbling back

4

across the roadway, Roger sprang to the ground and gained the front door of the menaced building in a series of well-weighted bounds. Here he faced about, red with effort and dark with wrath, in an attitude which could not be misunderstood.

"Zounds and death!" he thundered, breathlessly. "Men, men, what does all this mean?"

There was a disconcerted murmur. They were loth to make head against their oracle and their idol. There was not a man present but had been the recipient of his neighborly kindness, and derived a good share of his rather unreliable education from "General" Armstrong's "public day" disquisitions and discussions in the county town! They remembered, too, that he had stood unflinchingly by his political principles when those principles involved the danger of imprisonment or worse.

"It means, sir," at last answered the small, sharp-eyed man who led the party, touching his hat respectfully, but showing that he at least had quite recovered from his first dismay; "it means that we seen there was a viper yere, and we come down to stop his hissin'."

"Michael Garr," demanded Armstrong, severely, "have you no better brains than that? Do you want to see me and mine given over to execution and confiscation in order that you may take vengeance on a wretched demagogue? Do you remember the retaliations of 1863?"

Some of the party were evidently much struck by this suggestion; but Garr answered shrewdly—

"Ah, General, them days is gone; ye're mighty safe now."

"And you, John Simpson," exclaimed Armstrong. "I thought you were more of a man. Are you not ashamed to bring a party of twenty to kill a poor devil who is no match for one side of you?"

The huge man shifted his feet uneasily, but his quicker-witted comrade interposed with the remark: "I've seen more'n that after a *fox*, an' he hadn't done nothin' but steal chickens neither."

Roger remembered his early sports, and answered hastily, " Be civil, Garr." Then he added gently, to conciliate: " Foxes are foxes, and men are men."

"And devils are devils," retorted Garr. " 'Fore God, I say it's a blessed work to kill 'em."

" Look yander, Gineral," cried Simpson, thus egged on and pointing to the blood on the pavement—" that's *his* work. That man's wuss'n a devil. He's powerful mean. It's a mussy to stamp him out—*an' we're boun' to do it.*"

" Oh, boys, boys !" cried Roger Armstrong, in dire distress, as he realized the white heat of their determination. " Think what you are doing. Will you bring disgrace on your State ? —on old Accomac ?—on you and me, and all of us ? Come, I have not often asked favors at your hands, grant me this. Don't fear that I shall forget it. What, are there none of you who have ever had kindnesses from Roger Armstrong ? He is getting to be an old man now, and some of you are not so young as you were ; is there nothing in our long lives passed side by side which should give him a right to appeal to you as man appeals to man, and friend to friend ? See, our interests, our hopes are bound up together. Your shame is my shame, your glory my glory, your sin my sin. I will not pass into the presence of my God with the thought that I have let you soil your souls with this atrocious crime."

A hush fell for a moment on the now largely augmented crowd ; then turbulent murmurs began again ; and a stranger's voice called, " Haul the politician out of there."

"You lie !" roared Roger, from his vantage post. " Hand the rahscal up here who calls Roger Armstrong a politician. Where is he ?"

The fellow slunk off amid jeers ; and Simpson expressed the general opinion of the mob—

" Yes, he *does* lie, Gineral. You're the highest-toned gentleman on the Eastern Sho'. I'll vote fo' you, sir ; an' I'll fight fo' you ; but I can't do this fo' you. We all come to kill that Vamper ; an', 'fore God, you best get out of the way."

" Yes, out of the way!   Out of the way!   No time for talk!"
called a dozen impatient voices.

Armstrong answered with stern composure, but in a voice
so loud that it dominated all their uproar—

" I most assuredly shall do nothing of the kind.   You shall
not enter this door unless you pass over my dead body."

Again there was silence for a moment; then fiercer cries—

" Let him die if he wants to.   Stop talking, and clear the
way!"

" Well, if I must," observed Simpson, bringing his ponderous
right foot slowly up another step.

" Halt!" commanded Armstrong, in so emphatic a voice
that Simpson involuntarily stopped and half raised his hand to
his hat.

Before that pause ended, a third party interposed, a tall,
stately man with a broad panama hat, silky, brown beard, white
skin, and faultless attire.   Sitting in a front room of the hotel
he had watched with some interest the rout of the negroes; he
had even laid his mint julep aside to nod approval when he
saw the lynchers approach; but he had not thought of taking
part in the drama until he saw that a gentleman was in peril.
Then he tossed away his straw, drained his glass, flung on his
hat, and strode swiftly down to the rescue, cocking his revolver
as he came.   When he reached the side of Roger Armstrong
the face of John Simpson was directly before him, rising far
above the rest of the crowd.   With the single exclamation,
" You dog!" he fired full at that face.   The aim though quick
was deadly, but the bullet went harmlessly by overhead.   Armstrong had dashed up the hand of his champion.

" No," said he, with one of his beaming smiles, " John Simpson and I have been friends too long to kill one another;"
then changing his tone as he saw signs of irresolution in the
crowd, he called out with a prodigious assumption of authority—

" In the name of the State of Virginia, I command you to
disperse and return to your homes."

Michael Garr wheeled about and began elbowing his way back to his horse, observing astutely—

"I reckon it's all up, boys; come along."

Simpson stood a moment as if in a daze; then struck the butt of his gun on the steps with a great clang, and, turning half around, declared aloud—

"I can't hurt the Gineral, boys; an' I'll be blanked if any one else shall, either. Not as I'm afeard o' that dandy's pistol, nor——"

"Will you oblige me, sir, by stepping into the hall?" requested Mr. Armstrong, addressing Captain Hawksley, his new ally.

The latter bowed stiffly and retired a little beyond the doorway, where he stood, serene but vigilant, revolving in his mind whether he could with honor avoid calling out the man who had taken such a liberty with his person. He did not wish for a meeting; indeed he had just finished a tedious journey by rail undertaken for the purpose of visiting the offender and his niece; and he valued her approbation above all things. But there was a certain sense of duty in these matters; and it had always been the captain's way to treat his honor as a very sensitive plant. This was sometimes inconvenient, for the word included all the more finely spun ramifications of his reputation for courage, veracity, propriety, and fifty other things.

Yet he might very well have rested his case on what he had been and done. It was said that the war had produced no more capable or daring partizan leader, and now in peace . he was winning wide recognition as an original critic of current facts and public men, writing from a perversely peculiar standpoint and with a polished bitterness of style that reminded one of Randolph of Roanoke.

Mr. Armstrong broke this reverie by advancing radiantly with outstretched hand, exclaiming as he entered the hall, "By Zines, I never found so much difficulty in exerting my authority, sir. One of my best speeches would have been wasted on those fellows. You came just in time, and I thank you cordially, sir. I hope you will excuse my roughness, sir. Necessity was urgent."

Captain Hawksley weighed this apology conscientiously before accepting it. On the whole he thought it would do, as there had been no intention to affront. Having come to this wise conclusion, he was not disposed to be niggardly in response—especially as the other was beginning to look hurt and vexed.

"Certainly, sir," the captain answered; "I am especially proud to have been of service to *you*, Mr. Armstrong."

He was about to add more when an unpleasant voice added: "Second that motion." Turning, he confronted Ishmael Vamper.

The latter, when Armstrong first interposed in his behalf, had audibly wondered, "What's that old party's game?" The appeal for mercy had drawn from him the admiring comment, "If that don't fetch 'em, it's useless for *me* to try." When he heard Hawksley stride past, he cried, "Don Quixote No. 2!" with a ghastly grin into his looking-glass. Then realizing that he might do better by himself than to sit there whetting his wit on his desperate fortunes, he bowed to his grimacing reflected image with—"Now for the windmills! Let us warfare a little! Selah!" and opening the door, sauntered jauntily down in time to witness the *finale*.

Hawksley stared at him haughtily on hearing his volunteer "second;" and announced, "I'll have you remember, if you'll be so keind, that interruptions are distasteful."

Vamper would have liked to kill him; yet drew off without even a sneer. Ishmael's cold-blooded care of himself often seemed like cowardice.

Hawksley curled his lip in mistaken contempt, and Armstrong looked shame and pity. The two. latter had met before, and a seat behind the refractory black horse was offered and accepted with no need for introduction or explanation. Then Ishmael Vamper, quite unabashed, came to the front again, saying, "I am sure you would like the company of a man of saving grace; behold the candidate."

The planter answered frigidly—" There are only two seats, sir."

Vamper responded with mocking insistance: "Thanks for your consideration; but I've no false pride. I'll sit on the floor or in the lap of some good Samaritan. No cutlets out of Vamper for these cannibals! What ho, let's chariot a little."

What was to be done? The fellow was as obnoxious as he well could be; his very presence nauseated—yet he had asked for shelter. Wildly, preposterously no doubt, and with every aggravation of impudence; but nevertheless from a real danger, and one which there was no other probable means of avoiding. Cypress Beach had never refused this boon, and Mr. Armstrong felt that blood would be on his hands and his soul if harm ensued from refusing it now. So he groaned in spirit, but replied—

"You had better bring out a chair or stool for a seat."

Before starting, he insisted on seeing the wounded negroes duly cared for. In this work Vamper (followed by Captain Hawksley's amused contempt) was almost equally active. He began to gain favor in Mr. Armstrong's eyes.

"I will say one thing for you, Mr. Vamper," remarked the old gentleman, glad to find something to commend, "You are thoughtful for your injured followers."

Vamper thought there was a sly joke under the old man's kind exterior; and answered, willing to gain credit for astuteness—

"It goes without saying, *a la Francais,* that I shouldn't have done it if I hadn't thought they would recover. Three dead niggers—no help nor hurt there; but three live niggers doctored—three 'strikers' for your uncle—as the ungodly say— *savez?*"

Armstrong could not believe that the other was in earnest. Taking the word "striker" in its more ordinary significance, he asked—

"One word, sir, what is the objective point of your move-

ment, if I may ask? What do you want strikers for? A war
upon capital?"

"That's the ostensible object," replied Vamper; then with
a confidential leer: "But what in Tophet do I care for these
dogs of laborers? *I want an office!*"

Captain Hawksley uttered a low, musical laugh. Mr. Armstrong asked breathlessly—

"Is *that* your only object?"

"Yes, my lord," answered Vamper, airily. "'Victors,' you
know! 'Spoils,' you know! Office! Office! Let us officiate;" and he swept his right hand out and back with a
greedy, money-raking motion.

The elder man, holding himself in readiness for attack, burst
out with—

"Sir, you must be a scoundrel."

Vamper laughed aloud—

"What, have you just discovered that? The boarding-
house keepers of the North American continent found it out
long ago."

Roger Armstrong seemed about to fling him out of the
buggy; but was checked by Hawksley's deferential touch,
and the suggestion—

"Pardon me, but unhappily the thing is your guest."

"So he is, hang him," admitted Armstrong, dismally. Except an occasional meditative "zounds and death!" he kept a
most surprising silence for the next mile or so. Ishmael made
up for it by a constant flow of grotesque, boastful nonsense.
Captain Hawksley still watched and smiled; resolving that
Jessica should not long be annoyed by this phenomenon.

Suddenly a turn of the road revealed a crowd of negroes
around a meeting-house. They consisted mainly of the rem-
nants of the body just dispersed in Nodaway; and were now
awaiting reinforcements preparatory to—they knew not what.
The appearance of their leader, and as they supposed, his
captors gave them an immediate object. They pressed threat-
eningly into the carriage-way and around the vehicle under
the direction of a squat, ruffianly fellow, in whom Mr. Arm-

strong was surprised to recognize Mammy Charlotte's long-absent son, John.

" I think," suggested Hawksley, cocking his revolver and looking calmly at Vamper, "that it would be as well to explain matters, if you will be so keind."

The Captain clung tenaciously and patriotically to the Hebridean pronunciation common in most parts of Virginia. He would not have discarded a superfluous vowel on any account.

Vamper sneered inwardly, but lost no time in beginning the required statement. This time he chose a more grandiose style of oratory than usual, his object not being to excite but to console, allay, encourage, and please.

" Fellow citizens," said he, rising, " let me congratulate you on the successful issue of our grand rally for the great cause of man. Victory does not consist alone in the mere resistless onslaught of wronged numbers; though that too will come if the oppressors listen not to the warning which is borne on every breeze, if they heed not the blazon stamped on the broad earth and the eternal heavens. But the noblest victory is the victory over the hearts and minds of noble men, and *that* we have won to-day. I am going hence, not as a prisoner, but as the invited guest of the foremost man of all this region, a generous enemy, of whose final conversion to the cause of right his present manly action affords a glorious forecast. I must ask you to open the way for us."

Roger Armstrong had listened in bewilderment. How a man could throw so much sincerity into his words when there was none in his heart quite passed comprehension. He began to wonder whether the speaker were not after all a misled enthusiast, who took a morbid pleasure in maligning himself. But the final suggestion brought the old gentleman to his feet.

" Now *I* want a word with you," he announced. " Mr. Vamper's prognostication is without a shadow of foundation. I have told you before, and I tell you now, that you have too many privileges already. As a good citizen, I acquiesce in

accomplished facts, however deplorable, but I will not advo-
cate further unwise concessions. I talk to you frankly, for
that is the truest kindness. Some of you were raised on my
place, and many have been in my employ; have I ever treated
you unjustly or unkindly?" There were many negative
answers from different parts of the crowd. "Then," he continued, "I know you will take it to heart when I warn you
not to expect too much. A scientist, a great man at the
North, has recently discovered that the negro's head does not
possess a certain suture, as it is called, which allows the white
man's skull to expand, and his brain to grow. Hence, try as
hard as you may, your brains cannot develop beyond a certain extent. It is the will of God, for His own wise pur-
poses. You can never be the equals of white men in any
respect, and the effort to reverse the Divine decrees will only
bring a curse and destruction upon you. Therefore, you who
are well disposed, go quietly back to your homes, and count
upon me as your friend whenever you are in distress.

"To the few who seek in turmoil and confusion an opportunity for robbery and all baseness"—here his eye rested
sternly on the face of John, who stared back at him in stolid
defiance—"to that evil few I would give one reminder—the
whipping-post has been re-established. It is well not to for- ·
get." He sat down; bowed authoritatively; and drove on.

Ishmael Vamper looked at him derisively, and then back
for the benefit of the crowd. But he was surprised to find a
very unsympathetic response in their faces. The shadow of
old mastership was too much for him. His next glance at
Armstrong was one of admiration and longing.

"That 'suture' business was a trump," said he; "but how
did you dare play it? Can you really make the idiots swallow *anything?*"

"'Swallow! swallow!'" exclaimed Mr. Armstrong, in rising
wrath, "why, man, its God's truth. Zounds and death!"

Vamper had no faith in his rescuer's sincerity (or in anything
else); but was beginning to hate him with a deadly hatred for
his pretense of moral superiority.

CHAPTER VI.

"THERE WORKETH A SPELL."

Vamper possessed a natural aptitude for that obscure and uncanny art which we term mesmerism or animal magnetism a very real and dangerous endowment, however discredited in some quarters by the fraud and legerdemain which imitate it. The worst human passions had instigated him to develop this power; and they had been reinforced by the inhuman desire to drag down all things that men called high or pure and make a mock of them; until a superstitious person might well be excused for finding in him the evil eye of olden time witchcraft.

Jessica would have been in some peril from this influence at any time, by reason of the extreme responsiveness which underlay her Hebe-like charms, her social aptitude and girlish enjoyment. There are subtle weaknesses of nerve texture and current which may work a dreadful treason to other outlines than those of Egeria. And now she was in a peculiarly receptive mood. The nervousness caused by last night's want of rest had been aggravated by the anxiety consequent upon her uncle's departure, and the rumors which reached her from the village; while the unobtrusive attentions of Robert Chauncey, and Prince's efforts at diversion, had rather added to the strain by reminding her of the duty of self-control.

She welcomed her uncle with a kiss that conveyed all the enthusiasm of thankful relief; then turned with a happy smile to Captain Hawksley; and, lastly, greeted pleasantly (as intro-

duced) her new acquaintance, Mr. Vamper; though marvel-
ling at his presence not a little.   He took her hand and held it
longer and more tightly than custom quite warranted, flushing
her cheek and flooding her heart with an unknown feeling that
was much more than dismay.   As the others passed on, she
rallied her will desperately and looked up with an effort at
self-defense and repulsion; but her eyes fell again at once, and ·
she shook, breathing heavily.   The wild rabbit shocked into
bewildered paralysis by the sudden cry of many hounds—
though, oh, so willing to fly!—is not more helpless.

"I think we shall be very good friends," he said significantly.

"I hope so," she replied, dreamily, still shuddering.

He held her hand a moment longer, to be sure there was no
resistance; then quietly released it, and entered the house after
her.

While her uncle was introducing him to Mr. Chauncey, she
slipped off to her room; dropped breathlessly into a chair;
and bared her full fine arm to the elbow, looking attentively
along it from the ring.   Then she let it fall, and turned her
eyes on the sunlight which flecked the floor; thinking in a
dazed way.   Had she told the truth in saying she hoped they
would be friends?   What *was* the attitude of her soul, herself, toward him?   She had believed all her life that no man
whom she could ever meet as an equal would cross the magic
circle of a pure woman's rebuke; but she saw already that it
was less than a cobweb barrier to him.   Her traditions were
all cast to the winds, and her soul was trembling within her.
The fascination of fear was not all: she recognized the weirder
fascination of unlikeness—unlikeness not merely to the other
men whom she had met, but (as it seemed) to the essential
spirit of humanity itself.

The physical effort of her hurried toilet scattered these
shadows and half persuaded her that she could laugh at
them.   No doubt, however, there was a dash of uneasiness
in her defiant singing, as she went down the hall; for she
was not wont to be so demonstrative.

Her uncle's late success made him even more fluent than usual at the table, so they had over again the well-worn story of the Pennsylvanian who called a handsome horse "ugly" when he meant that it was vicious, and the one about the Quaker who preached negro equality to a pursuing slave-owner, yet refused to purchase the runaway's freedom by accepting him for a son-in-law. These and many more were strung on a thread of moralizing which set all human experience and political philosophy at defiance. Yet he was so sure of being right in his genial wrong-headedness that the hearer often began to doubt whether the solid foundations of the universe *were* solid after all.

The meal ended, Hawksley was carried off to inspect the farms and stock. Chauncey, faintly smiling, as one who sees without grief a remembered weariness pass to a rival's shoulders, turned with dissembled reluctance to keep an appointment which had been pressed upon him by the politely assiduous little Prince. Vamper declined both parties almost curtly. Before Jessica could frame a plan for escape, he had laid claim to her services as entertainer; and the others had departed, vexed indeed to leave her in such unworthy company, but with no serious misgiving.

The grim cloud had been lifted from Jessica's mind in the normal life of the last hour or so; but now as she sat in the curtain-dimmed parlor, with its quaint furniture and quainter faded portraits, there came upon her, like a warning from another world, a vehement impulse to flee. When the voices of her friends had died utterly away outside in the deathlike hush of the country, this instinct overpowered even her keen sense of propriety, and she half rose. As she did so, she felt the keen eyes of Vamper mocking her perturbation. Her over-dread of ridicule checked her for a moment. Before it passed, the desire to go seemed to fade away.

Turning to the picture album (what safer in its conventionalism) she fluttered, trying to keep her usual tone—

"Ah, Mr. Vamper, I am going to show you some pretty girls. You mustn't dare to contradict me"

"I shouldn't," he responded dryly. "Wheresoever the ladies and gentlemen are gathered together, we know who must obey. Bring on the girls."

She stepped to the table not over pleased (for the volume was heavy and his tone both dominant and nonchalant), yet in truth not daring to refuse. Her tremor as she reached forward caused The Lady's Ring to strike against a grotesquely wrought silver bell, with a keen menacing note like the cry of a soul in pain. She started back echoing it.

Vamper stepped beside her, asking—

"Ha; a mouse or a goblin?"

"It—startled me," she gasped. "It does not sound so—to everything. It—came from the North—Salem—long ago. They tell——" and she looked at him, like one battling, with furtive query and fright.

"Ah, a wizard-finder's toy," he answered, ringing it fantastically; "order up the witches."

Smiling Susan appeared in the doorway.

"Did you ring fo' me, Miss Jessie?" she asked.

"Not any," Vamper answered for her; but the negress lingered. Did she see anything in her young mistress's face which urged her not to go away? A hesitating expression troubled the dense sunshine of her countenance for a moment. Then she withdrew it, still grinning, and closed the door.

Jessica, seating herself submissively beside Vamper, pointed out and named one portrait after another; while he, delighting in cat-and-mouse tactics, encouraged her growing sense of something like security by a droll running commentary, that made hidden faults and foibles start into unnaturally vivid relief. More than once it cheated her into her usual mellow laugh.

Her voice had almost its old clearness as she pointed to an exceptionally beautiful and intelligent face, asking—

"Do you find anything unlovely *there?*"

Vamper's lip twitched with expectant amusement, as he answered—

"She *is* pretty; but not so sweet as—Jessica."

The young lady could not but remember that this was the very bit of presumption which she had so pointedly forestalled only yesterday when threatened by her intimate friend, Mr. Chauncey. She had always been almost excessively particular with regard to these matters of etiquette and minor ceremonial. So she straightened herself, as in duty bound, but with a dismayed consciousness of the odds against her.

"I never allow," she began; but she could get no further. His eyes made her droop and shrink like a wilted plant, and the words turned to mere quiverings of the lips.

"Of course not, they never do," he replied. "But all the same, Jessica, I think you won't prude with me, Jessica. My Euphrosyne—'goddess fair and *free!*'—'buxom, blithe and debonair!'—as a certain blind party has it."

While he spoke his right hand closed on hers, and his left, emphasizing the words, stroked lightly up over and beyond the soft, fine wrist that her flowing sleeve uncovered. Her cheeks, which had paled, flushed again painfully at this; but there was no other motion and no sound. He paused, in keen-eyed enjoyment of her distress; then saying, "'Sweet,' eh?—let us test," bent his face over till his lips approached her own.

At that crisis, a quick patter of hoofs came up the carriage-way; there was a sudden grind of turning wheels on the gravel, and a deep voice announced—

"I should have struck him a most awful blow."

Mr. Armstrong was explaining what would have happened to Simpson the forester, if the latter had persisted. His arrival sent Vamper back out of line with the windows, cursing half audibly.

It brought still further relief to Jessica. Her uncle had a way of jotting down his farming statistics on odd fragments of paper, and then shedding them about over the house like snowflakes. This time he fancied that one of the flakes had drifted into her room; and requested her to see whether it could be found. She rose, bowing acquiescence with rather a dazed air, and passed out. The last words that reached her were (in his most Olympian tones), " Slavery, sir, is as necessary to a gentleman as rain is to corn." She had heard this sonorous exordium often before ; but now it had a personal application which made her lean against the wall and fight for breath.

Reaching her room, she turned the key and fell over upon the bed, where she lay for a long time without moving. Her mind worked as though in a dense fog and under a brain-crushing weight. She was conscious of a desolate sense of having lost the defensive power of womanhood. She knew that she was absolutely at Vamper's mercy—or whatever attribute might be supposed to take its place—and that he had deprived her not only of the power to reveal her danger and implore aid, but even of any clearly defined wish to do either. His mastery seemed so inevitable, so irreversibly established that (horrible as the idea would ordinarily have seemed to her) she could not even be sure whether it were right or wrong. Of one thing alone she could be certain ; her heart was so far from feeling any affection for her tyrant, that it would have turned to God in thankfulness at the news of his death. Nothing remained but to keep up the artificialities of life, and drift, dumbly moaning.

She was still lying thus when a servant rapped to announce " Marse Roger make his complimumps, an' would be much 'bleege' fo' dat slip o' paper ; an' supper moughty near ready."

Luckily, the memorandum was near at hand. Jessica thrust it out, and began her toilet. When she descended all the men thought that her apparel and coiffure had never showed to better advantage. But both Captain Hawksley and Robert Chauncey were conscious of an inexplicable something in her manner which filled them with disquiet. ˙ Even when bridling with her little bird-like motions, it was evident that she had no longer the bird's blithe certainty of wing. The lovers were far enough from suspecting the truth, but each resolved to bring his tantalizing courtship to a climax before another day had passed, and win some definite answer for good or ill.

CHAPTER VII

"RIDE, BOLDLY RIDE."

Roger Armstrong had not the least suspicion of the dire evil that menaced his roof, and he did not find it easy to ask any one to leave that shelter. But he had received warnings which compelled some action for Vamper's own sake. The animosity of the more dangerous citizens was still unappeased, and although the agitator was safe at Cypress Beach, who could guarantee his life in any chance stroll through the neighboring woods or along an unfrequented road?

With this thought in his mind, Roger Armstrong the next morning invited Vamper to ride with him. This would have been an unwelcome suggestion at any time, but Ishmael found it especially irksome now that he had been so long practically excluded from Jessica's company—indeed ever since the return of her Uncle and Hawksley the day before. So he impudently feigned lassitude, and answered in the slang of the day, "Oh, give us a rest."

The host bit his lip: "I have important business with you, sir," said he.

Vamper, thus enforced, rose with a quizzical look of distress, saying, "As a sheep before the shearers."

After they had driven a little way Mr. Armstrong turned and said—

"Mr. Vamper, you are in danger."

"Well-l, I *might* be in a bumble-bee's nest," was the philosophical reply.

"The people are excited against you," urged the other,

5

anxiously. "The boat for Baltimore leaves our wharf at
noon. I must advise you to take it—on your own account,
sir."

"Oh, doubtless," replied Vamper, with half-veiled irony;
"but don't solicitude overmuch. I have left *several* places
unanimously and *in toto*. Let us procrastinate."

"Confound him!" ejaculated Armstrong, inwardly; "How
am I *ever* to get rid of the rahscal? And he certainly *will* be
put to death." Then he fell to wondering, as others had
wondered, whether all this distortion of the English language
and human nature grew out of something which might lessen
responsibility. At last he answered resignedly, "If you get
into trouble remember you had full monition."

When they returned, Jessica was away, and Vamper learned
that she had made a second engagement for the afternoon·
However, there were but a given number of hours of day, so
he braced his patience to carry him through them in the
character of a sardonic loiterer and general tormentor. Long
before sundown every small African about the premises had
come to regard him with a peculiar terror, and Prince's lordly
indignation had more than once almost choked him, though
the boy returned resolutely again and again to the task of
entertaining this intolerable guest.

Almost immediately after Vamper had been carried away
as related, Jessica had declared vivaciously that she must
make a shopping-raid on the main street of Nodaway. This
was partly the result of a strong impulse to get as far from
him as possible; partly of a feverish, half-recognized yearning to make the most of life's sunshine, before a horror settled
upon it.

Of course there were two volunteers on the instant. She
looked at them with a comical affectation of dismay.

"What both!" she cried; then, clapping her hands, "I
have it. You shall draw lots, and the loser shall be my
escort this evening to the old church at Nyington Roads. I
have been longing and longing to see it again."

Captain Hawksley felt that this appeal to chance was hardly decorous; and he liked it even less when the result went against him. However, he had the grace to show no more than a playful chagrin. After the others departed, he sauntered down to the cove where Prince was fishing. The two were fast friends already; for the boy rejoiced in this new mine of stirring anecdotes; and the duellist soldier did not easily weary of narrating them to one who showed so many of his own qualities in embryo.

Several of these tales had already been repeated as they lounged in their boat, moored just within the edge of the cypress shade, when Prince seemed to feel that it was his turn to say something startling.

"Captain," he announced, "I am going to shoot a man to-night."

"The deuce you are!" opening his eyes at this practical application of his doctrines, "and whom may it be? Don't pick any quarrel, my boy."

"Oh, there ain't any quarrel. It's only a chicken-thief."

"Ah! I see—you mean the fellow that broke into the hen-house last night."

This, by the way, was Vamper's lieutenant, John, who had taken to feeding at once his spite and his constitution at Mr. Armstrong's expense.

"You're mighty right, Captain," answered Prince.

"Then I advise you not to lose any sleep on his account. Thieves don't visit the same place two nights in succession."

"You don't know *our* thieves, Captain," persisted Prince, with a wise air.

The tolerably experienced Hawksley began laughing gently to himself, then stopped suddenly.

"I beg your pardon, Prince," he said; "you're a capital little gentleman, and have my sincere regyards. But, all the same, you had better sleep indoors to-night, and save your powder for the squirrels."

Prince's brow cleared; but he did not promise.

Meanwhile Jessica and Chauncey were cantering on briskly down the gently undulating road.   There was not much connected conversation at first, for he could spare very little attention from the arduous duty of managing his horse and keeping reputably in his saddle.   Jessica was not usually inconsiderate in her treatment of escorts ; but this time, half in abnormal superficial gaiety, half in a blind and most unjust yearning to punish somebody, she certainly made his hard lot very much harder.

Nevertheless they entered the village decently.   She pointed out to him the little court-house, with a queer grouping of agricultural machines in front and a rude wooden fence around all ; the bazaar-like row of small shops ; the plethoric brick tavern, with its sickly "temperance" competitor ; the bank ; the sparsely tenanted, unguarded jail ; and the streets lined with incongruous dwelling-houses, generally crowded down to the pavement in a city-emulating fashion which robbed the place of a good part of its shady rural beauty.   While she made her purchases, he amused himself by watching the long shabbily-clad countrymen of the poorer class slouching about the corners and doorways, the few weightily-stepping clear-voiced farmer magnates in their faded, careless apparel ; the negro gossippers to whom the recent disturbance and bloodshed had already become a godsend, in the way of anecdote and reminiscence, rather than a portent and a thing of dread.   He was surprised to see how many vehicles containing articles of some value were standing unwatched about the village.

Then his mind passed to certain things which he wished to say.   How should he begin ?   The choice of language ought to have been easy, for he had tested almost every conceivable formula of that sort in his sentimental episodes.   But this morning he was not aided by that thorough sympathy of the audience which draws forth an orator's happiest efforts.   If success were coming, somehow he did not feel it   But what was to be effected by waiting ?   Hawksley—that mispronouncing grindstone-hearted guerrilla—was more likely to gain ground with the lapse of time than to lose it. The man's hard daring, his record of physical and mental prowess, his tenacious adherence to what most people deemed hopeless, his perfect mastery of those out-door accomplishments in which Jessica herself excelled, gave him obvious advantages in the race. Robert's skill with the pencil, the brush, the springing foot, the vibrant cord, and the accurately modulated tone would go for nothing in comparison. And yet—and yet—he knew that he had not a ridiculous trait. It was very bitter.

While returning, they halted for a moment to breathe their horses in the shade of a wide-spreading oak that grew on a little knoll. The delicate fragrance of wild grape blossoms came from a thicket near by. A mocking-bird dropped lightly on a branch overhead, and rioted in a wild and varying melody. When he ceased and flew away, one or two cat-birds took up a less mellow and versatile, but still musical song. Flowers bloomed all along the roadside; and the whole landscape seemed to rejoice in its bath of sunlight.

Robert Chauncey had just devised a form of declaration in keeping with this environment, and promising the most joyous results, when Jessica unwittingly sealed his lips by demanding speech.

"Mr. Chauncey *used* to be an entertaining escort," said she, half tossing her head archly. "Ah, well, I suppose the peninsula air is bad for eloquence."

"Hardly," answered Chauncey, with a sudden revulsion to bitterness. "I notice the Captain finds it suits his 'gyarden' of rhetoric, 'regyardless' of English. You know——"

"I know," interrupted Jessica, with decision and some heat, "that Captain Hawksley is thoroughly a *man*. He has more than a drawing-room record."

Chauncey, piqued, responded with caustic deliberation—

"No; *blood stains* are inconvenient in drawing-rooms."

"Some of our city young men are in no danger of leaving

blood stains," she replied, curling her lip; "no, not if they were to bleed to death."

She turned from him humming scornfully.

Chauncey checked the first answer which rose from his heart. He was strangely disappointed in her. Had she shown such rudeness a few months sooner, his course would have been plain. But now he could not contemn her as merely vulgar, and seek a less faulty charmer. Besides, the good taste of his own remarks about his absent rival would not bear very close examination.

When at last he spoke, it was simply to say—

"All of which means that you think I have no spirit. Perhaps you may see cause to change your mind."

His unusual tone touched her. She turned quickly towards him, holding out her hand and saying—

"Let us be friends. I would not let *him* criticise *you* in your absence."

The truce was ratified, and they rode home in all comradeship; but the momentous words remained unspoken. He fancied a lurking contempt under every kindly phrase. And was this all that his assiduous attentions, his varied talents, his irreproachable gentleness had called forth? The spark of self-dissatisfaction already noted was fanned into a blaze.

Another now—and such another!—required credentials of his manhood. He resolved again and again that they should be forthcoming.

After dinner Captain Hawksley rode with Jessica to the old church. This half-ruinous, colonial relic stood in the midst of a cluster of massive oaks, looking out rather grimly across an estuary and the broad reach of Chesapeake Bay. Ivy crawled over it, forming a thick garment in many places. Here and there the quaint legend and sculpture of a time-defaced tombstone showed above the sod. No human dwelling was very near; no human voice broke the silence. The birds, the grass, the sky, and the great bay had not changed with the changing centuries. They were again with that cumbrous, quaintly caparisoned, dream-like past, which one cannot think on without a smile of affectionate regret.

She sat on the grassy terrace to which time had transformed the well-worn circular carriage-way; he, standing beside her, leaned against a large tree which grew out of its deepest hollow. Notwithstanding his affectionate hopes of a domestic future—indeed partly because of them—Captain Hawksley always treated Jessica with marked ceremony. Perhaps nothing else so greatly aided his suit.

"Yes," said he, continuing his thoughts aloud, "here your ancestors talked, and walked, and breathed, and laughed, and worshipped in those kyindly old days which it is our mission and our duty to bring back to earth."

She shook her head sadly—

"I fear that can never be."

"It is worth trying," he replied; "men lived then, as they were intended to live, in good will with those around them, and in patriarchal rule over the servants born on their land. No desire then to overturn the divinely established order of things. A time when no one questioned the supremacy of chivalric honor! A time when the truths of revelation were unassailed by cavilling!

"And why should it not return? Do you remember, Miss Armstrong, De Tocqueville's weighty words, 'Nothing has so great a fixity of purpose as an aristocracy'? That is true even when the aristocracy, acting from instinct, does not clearly know what its purpose *is*. The South has not cast away her ideals, nor have her sons lost their manhood. In the fullness of time her ascendency will surely come."

"In good truth, I wish it *might*," she answered.

"Meantime, continued he, "we have our lands, our homes with their ancestral associations, our white adherents who have not yet learned to throw off their traditional reliance on gentlemen; our negroes, who need only the pressure of a firm hand (and a lavish one) to subside into their proper station. We can brighten our neglected gyardens, restore these antique

places of worship to their former solemn beauty, and show in
the lives of ourselves and our families that the decorum, the
nobility, and the frank, pure affection of old days have not vanished from earth.   We can revive the good old custom of love,
Miss Armstrong, in an age of lawless vagary and mercenary
self-seeking."

There was a beseeching tremor in his last words, which
showed how deeply the man's soul had entered into the dreams
of which he spoke.   They appealed almost as strongly to every
enthusiasm of the young girl's nature.   She felt that the very
effort to attain them was an exaltation.   The romantic zealot
beside her seemed incomparably heroic.   She felt a real longing to share his aims, his hopes, his life.

Yet she sat silent, with a cloud on her brow and more than
a cloud on her brain and heart.   A chill horror struck through
her very love.   She could not clearly distinguish whence it
came.   Was there something within her soul like a malignant
alien personality?

For a moment her lethargic will was quickened as if a great
cry went through her, and she struggled as one struggles with
the nightmare, though no limb stirred.   She knew perfectly
how very near she was to all the delight of freedom.   One
frank sentence, one word, one hint, and the unholy bondage
would be speedily shattered—with the bodily frame of him
who had imposed it.   Yet there was little hope in her striving.
The very effort seemed to make more vivid that sensation of a
jeering, dominant presence; and suddenly her hand made an
involuntary motion of withdrawal as though something hurt it.

She closed her eyes for a minute, then rose with a bewildered air, and hurried from a conflict which was turning into
torment her few remaining hours of self-deceitful happiness.
Yet even while she did so, that happiness seemed to her unspeakably ghastly.   She would have prayed if she could.

Captain Hawksley had drawn no comfort from her puzzling
changes of expression; and her final action filled him with a
desolate sense of rejection embittered by unkindness.   Never-

theless, he assisted her to mount, and rode homeward dutifully, though silently, by her side.

As they neared Cypress Beach, she brightened rather per-
functorily, and said—

"We make quite a Doresque picture—we and our long
shadows, with these dead trees and cypresses.

"A picture!" said he, politely rallying his attention. "Yes,
I remember to have seen one of his engravings which is something like it; but the personages there were a lady and her
champion journeying toward an enchanter's den." After a
pause, he added, "There is always, I suppose, some sort of
truth at the bottom of these old myths."

This platitude was uttered for lack of something fresher or
wiser; and he was surprised to see Jessica's face shine for an
instant afterward, as though a hope had flashed out of its tomb.

CHAPTER VIII.

"ALL THE BLESSEDNESS OF SLEEP."

The household at Cypress Beach dispersed earlier than usual that night. Jessica walked to her room, and sat down wearily. The enforced brightness of the evening had left her face, and an indefinable set look had come instead. It was as though her soul had been stolen.

By and by she loosened and removed her shoes; then sank back in her chair, and sat quite still again. She heard all the human sounds of the house die away one by one. She saw the last reflected lamplight disappear from the lawn and the trees. She waited yet longer till sleep settled heavily upon Cypress Beach. Then came the time which she had known all along *would* come.

There was no signal to eye or ear, yet a hempen rope could not have drawn her more surely. She stepped, without volition, to the door, opened it cautiously, and passed silently through the halls down the old staircase, and out at the half-open front door. Turning aside, she approached the dense shadow of a linden tree, doubly dark in that sparsely starlit night. A storm was racing up from the west with mutterings of thunder, and flushes, rather than flashes, of lightning.

Before she had quite passed under the tree, she felt her hand clasped; but could neither shrink nor shudder as the deathly thrill crept up her nerves. Then Vamper's voice congratulated her on her promptness. She felt him draw her toward him—helpless, will-less, breathless!

He had spoken in a plainly audible voice, knowing that nothing less than shouting was likely to waken the sleepers within the house, and not being aware of any watcher outside.

In almost instant response, a boyish voice at no great distance cried out, "Aha, I've got you now!" and Vamper started back as if expecting a shot. Jessica rushed toward the house. Almost in her pathway she descried a dim figure levelling a gun at her. "Prince!" she shrieked; and simultaneously a flash of lightning from the now nearly overhanging storm threw them both into strong relief.

As soon as the crash and echoing of thunder ceased, the boy began—

"Why, Cousin Jessie, why! I'm mighty glad I didn't fire. I didn't suspect it was you. Does your voice ever sound like a man's? I disremember——Well!"

The last exclamation was caused by her disappearance. She did not pause till she reached her own room, breathing like a hunted doe. A sense of unmerited shame fairly overcame her. Beyond this she was in a medley of emotions. Would Prince tell! *What* would he tell? Might it not be best if he did? Exposure would be very dreadful; but nothing could be so bad as this hovering of surely settling sin. Great vistas of deepening shade and multiplying terror stretched out into her future as she thought. Was there any whiteness of her soul, any innermost sanctuary of self, which might hope to escape desecration? With such uncannily deft and knowing hands (delighting in the work) to urge and drag, and snare and weary her poor disheartened, fitfully liberated, human will, who could say how or when the uncertain line might be passed which separates helpless yielding from measurably responsible volition. No backward steps *then;* no salvation! She strove to kneel; but she could not either in body or spirit. Did God really give over human souls to devils?

Her last thought, as she passed into a disordered slumber, was that the throbbing in her finger (due perhaps to the day's almost continuous horseback exercise) was a demon-dance in the depths of the great flame-panting gem which she could not discard (for more than a conventional restraint was upon her now)—that gem which had brought down from a long dead past the message and the menace of an undying sin.

CHAPTER IX.

"GOOD AT NEED."

Prince was puzzled and disquieted, but his faith in Jessica would not suffer him to suspect anything disgraceful or humiliating. He thought the matter over after the rain had driven him indoors; and decided with precocious considerations to keep silence, and to avoid anything which might even seem like watching her. There was more of affection and family pride than curiosity in Prince's composition.

Meanwhile an equally devoted friend was (more wisely) bestirring herself in Jessica's cause.

Soon after dawn, the young lady heard a gentle tapping at her door, and the voice of Mammy Charlotte saying "Miss Jessie."

"Come in, Mammy," was the languid response.

Mammy Charlotte was certainly nearer to a comprehension of the case than any one else at Cypress Beach. Love had sharpened her perceptions, and Vamper (underrating mulatto acuteness) had taken no special pains to mask his proceedings from her. She had noticed Jessica's involuntary head-turnings and glances, and Vamper's expression of concentrated will and exultant half-smile. Indeed these last had seemed to recur even when Jessica was away on her afternoon ride, and the old nurse had been vastly relieved by the little lady's return—safe though clearly in an abnormal condition. Moreover, she had met her son John on the evening before, and had gleaned no little terror from his vague, boastful hints of his "boss's" occult power. She had brooded over these thoughts at night, until, out of gloomy thoughts and dire traditions, an unearthly figure reared itself in her imagination. It has borne many names in many lands. She called it— "Conjure."

Her object that morning was to investigate the matter by a candid loving talk with her young mistress. As she entered, the first things she saw were Jessica's stockings stained with earth and blood, and torn where sharp sticks had pierced them in her hurried flight. Mammy Charlotte stooped with a low exclamation of dismay, and then raised them one at a time, shaking her head. For a moment there was utter horror in her mind. "Miss Jessie," was all she could say.

The young girl, utterly unstrung, only covered her face moaning. This tended to confirm Charlotte's worst fears; but she drew near and laid her hand tenderly on the fine head with its wealth of tangled hair. "Honey," she asked, in a hushed, shaken voice, "is it too late?"

Jessica shook her head.

Mammy Charlotte breathed more freely.

"No, thank de Lord, *dat* couldn't be. He wouldn't 'low no such dessiccation. But can't you tell me about it, hon': I wants to help you."

Jessica's bosom heaved; her hands went down; her face was contorted with effort; a look of intense fright and despair came into her eyes; and she gasped, "I—I *can't.*" Then she turned over with a changed expression, saying peevishly, "There now, *do* leave me."

The old woman sighed, but passed out and busied herself in removing all traces of the night's adventure. While doing so, she thought out several plans of relief. She could not bring herself to adopt any which would endanger Jessica's good name.

When the latter came down to breakfast, she had need of all the inertia of past training and experience, to present a calm and conventional exterior. Almost the first words that she heard threatened trouble.

As her cousin appeared, Captain Hawksley asked him with forced jocoseness : "Well, Prince, did you have any luck in your sport last night?"

She listened anxiously, hardly knowing what she wished.

"No, sir," answered Prince, though with rather a conscious look, "I didn't get to shoot at 'em. This waiting in the rain for thieves is mighty indifferent fun. I shan't try it again, Captain."

Jessica could not misunderstand the emphasis laid on the last sentence, though he looked sedulously away from her; and she felt grateful accordingly. There was even a certain relief in the postponement of a crisis. Any conceivable outcome of the present complications was very dreadful.

The rest of the party began to rally Prince on his newly developed dread of hardship. Jessica saw his easily kindled displeasure mounting to his eyes, and flushing his cheek, and she had opened her lips to interfere, when she saw her uncle summoned to the door. Presently an exclamation from him cut short a mumbled message; and he came hastily travelling back with his heavy oscillating tread.

"I beg pardon for not waiting to see you off, Mr. Chauncey," said he, holding out his hand. "But I have just been advised that one of my finest horses is almost in the pangs of dissolution. I trust you will make allowance for my scant politeness, which is at the mercy of adverse circumstances."

"Certainly! certainly!" replied Chauncey. "Don't let me detain you a minute. You may be in time to save the poor brute."

"Is it possible that you are going to leave us!" said Jessica to Chauncey.

"I must," he answered; "that official quill of mine trembles in the balance."

"Those public moneys!" exclaimed Vamper, clasping his hands with an affectation of rapture. "Let us officiate. Let us deplete."

The words were unpleasantly meant, for Ishmael had acquired a supplemental hostility to the spruce young fellow who so easily outshone him in several directions. Moreover, he could read through Robert Chauncey's easy indifference of manner; and the contempt, which grew out of a refined taste, somehow came home to him a little more nearly than the contempt which grew out of honor or manhood.

Chauncey ate on composedly, but with a perceptible line of vexation between the eyes. Jessica hastened to say her few gracious words of regret; but rather lamely, for she was not at all sure that she wished him to stay. She hardly knew what she wished about anything or anybody.

Robert Chauncey, on his part, felt that life at Cypress Beach had become insupportable. It was bitter to think that he left no void behind; bitterer still to see his most dangerous rival left in full possession of the field (for Vamper did not count); yet nothing would be gained by remaining. Indeed, his best hope lay in some possible opportunity to show Jessica that there were capabilities in him which she could not contemn and might be proud of. But he saw no chance to distinguish himself in Accomac.

He was very willing to part from the other men. Even if they had not been rivals, he never could have liked Captain Hawksley. All mobile temperaments find something repellant in these persistent, statuesque natures which are sure to be ten years hence just what they were ten years ago, and which are forever certain of being exactly in the right. The man's enthusiasms were such as Chauncey could not share in any degree; and he stood aghast before such unrelenting earnestness of purpose and preposterous recalcitrancy of aim. They were as incomprehensible as Roger Armstrong's sudden transitions from barbaric roaring to truest courtesy; or Ishmael Vamper's inhuman selfishness and grotesque love of evil. Robert Chauncey was going back to those whom he *could* understand, and who could understand him.

CHAPTER X.

"ST. MICHAEL AND THE DRAGON."

As Mr. Armstrong placed his foot on the step of the buggy he heard his name called; and turned, to see Mammy Charlotte making toward him rheumatically.

"Zounds and death, woman!" he exclaimed, in a fury of impatience; "What *do* you want?"

She saw his unfitness to hear; but her need was urgent. Struggling hard with the necessity for conciseness, the pains in her back and limbs, and her shortness of breath, she began confusedly—

"Marse Roger—I want—tell you—Mr. Vampire——"

"Hang Mr. Vamper!" he replied, beginning to climb.

But she persisted: "Marse Roger 'ndeed——"

"*Must* you tell me now, Charlotte?" he cried, with a queer hopelessness of tone.

"Indeed——"

"Then in with you!—in with you and tell me as we go," he exclaimed, fairly hustling her into the vehicle as he spoke, and clambering rapidly after. They drove off at a surprising rate of speed. He was in one of his instantaneous moods (which almost always had some sort of relation to his sacred horseflesh), and nothing but lightning would satisfy him.

This was very disconcerting to Mammy Charlotte's plans. She had determined to guard Miss Jessie night and day, and now every moment whirled her farther and farther from Cypress Beach.

" Marse Roger," she petitioned, as soon as she could; " I wish you'd let me 'light."

" By Zines, Charlotte," he replied, excitedly, " I can't stop now. But what did you want to tell me ?"

She hesitated a moment, fearing to say too much; then spoke out boldly—

" Marse Roger, I wish Mr. Vampire would go away."

"Good Lord, so do I ! Is that all ?"

"Then why don't you *send* him away, Marse Roger ?"—feeling at the same time that she was taking a prodigious liberty.

He looked at her as if she were about to be transformed.

" Well !" said he.

After a while he asked gravely—

" Did you ever know of anybody being sent away from Cypress Beach ? Do you think that would be hospitable, Charlotte ?"

" I don't believe in no hospitality to a dessiccation," she answered doggedly.

"A what ?" asked he, forgetting in his amusement all about the dying horse, but still driving on, mechanically and like Jehu.

"A dessication, sir," she replied; " there didn't ought to be no conjure in Cypress Beach, Marse Roger."

He leaned back in his seat and laughed long and loudly, with a world of side-shaking, and an occasional interjected " Good Lord !" or " Zines and Death !" At last he commanded himself sufficiently to say—

" The desecration will be terminated soon, Charlotte. He will leave us in a day or two—your conjurer."

Here he broke down again in a fit of laughter at the delusion of this patient retainer, whose faith was not a whit shaken by his ridicule.

His mirth and her captivity ended suddenly. One of the buggy wheels, which had long been rickety, gave way with a crash, and after a few seconds of pitching and dragging, both

6

the occupants of the vehicle found themselves in the road.
Mr. Armstrong's hands still held the reins, anchoring the horse
securely. As usual, he was not much damaged, owing to the
solidity of his frame, his firmness of muscular texture, and his
full cushioning of softer material. Charlotte, who struck upon
him (thankfully) as she fell, declared afterward that she did not
feel a bone.

"This," he remarked, sitting bolt upright like a Japanese
idol, " is a most untoward incident."

No one contradicting the oracle, he continued—

"That wheel has been very bad for a long time, but it is a
most indifferent article now."

His companion gazed at it ruefully without a word, as she
stood rubbing herself.

"Charlotte!" he called to her, as if suddenly waking, and in
a tone that made her start, " run up to Mason's house yonder—
d'you hear—and tell him to come down and help me."

The overseer's house referred to was fully a quarter of a
mile up a side-road leading to the river; so some time passed
before she delivered her message. Then she rested a little and
reflected. Should she hobble wearily back to the buggy and
await its very doubtful return, with only a choice between sub-
sequent capricious abduction and an interminable homeward
journey down the road on foot? She could render no real
assistance to " Marse Roger," and was quite in despair of ob-
taining any help from him without disclosing what must be
kept secret for " Miss Jessie's" sake. The very thought of that
loved name and its owner's peril, drove her, like an external
impulsion, instantly into what she had been dimly foreseeing
and moaning over for at least ten minutes—a painful cross-
country tramp to the head of the cove at Cypress Beach. The
unusual exercise over the rough fields racked her joints unspeakably; but she held up and kept on.

At last, when the cove was nearly reached, she could go no
further. She saw two figures come out of the house and move
down toward a boat. In the taller she recognized Captain

Hawksley, in the other, Mr. Chauncey. She understood that the Virginian's courtesy had led him (in Mr. Armstrong's absence) to escort his rival to the steamboat (with no sense of the irony involved in that service); and that an easily-guessed influence had prevented Jessica from accompanying them. "Marse Roger" stranded far away, the visitors just departing, herself exhausted in the field, nobody at home for at least the next half-hour except the "conjurer" and his victim! Mammy Charlotte gasped and chilled as her mind ran over the facts which made up the situation. Then new life came to her limbs, and she hurried over the remaining space. Chauncey had just taken his seat in the boat, and Hawksley was about to step in after him, when she caught the latter by his sleeve with the single breathless imploring word—

"Don't!"

He turned to see who obstructed him, and when he found that it was a negress, shook off her hand as if it had been pollution. Then the instense solicitude of her face, and the thought that after all she was Miss Armstrong's old-time nurse, made him ask with some little unbending—

"What is the matter, my good woman?"

The captain was not altogether a favorite with Charlotte. She was very ready to admit the claims of the dominant caste, especially of the "quality;" but she thought that they should be assumed as inherent in the nature of things, and requiring no more assertion or even perception than the act of breathing. That was Marse Roger's habitual attitude in his relations with the colored people. Now, Captain Hawksley either arrogated or condescended, and this made the recognition of divine right more difficult. But at present she could think only of succor for her young mistress, so she uttered desperately and piteously the words—"Miss Jessie *wants* you, sir."

The woman's hysterical excitement almost defeated itself. Captain Hawksley looked doubtfully at her, and asked—

"Are you sure? It is only a few moments since we left her."

But Charlotte urged—

"*Do* go, sir. *Don't* wait, sir! *Do* go!" and sank dizzily down, still pointing toward the house.

Hawksley began to surmise that something must be really wrong; but he hesitated to abandon his companion. The latter, stung by what he thought Jessica's indelicate indication of preference at the very instant of his own departure, and blinded by jealousy to all else, struck in ironically—

"Oh, don't mind me! For heaven's sake don't keep the young lady waiting. Pull off, Noah!"

Before the captain could get ready his retort, the boat was several lengths from the shore, and still speeding outward. Too dignified to call after it, but swelling with wrath which must have an outlet, Hawksley wheeled, as if on parade, and strode rapidly toward the house. On the way an uncomfortable sensation, as though something shadowy and malignant lay in wait for him, came into his mind.

The course he took brought him to the crest of a little mound which afforded a view of the interior of the secluded library. His first glance into the latter brought him to a standstill. He saw two heads bent slightly away from him, the feminine one in a passive, listening attitude. Was he the spectator of a secret lovers' interview?—and one party to it the very woman whom *he* loved! Decidedly he must call out Vamper that afternoon; yet he could not stand there playing the spy. But as he was about to withdraw, old Charlotte's words, "Miss Jessie *wants* you," came back to him with a new meaning; and he paused irresolutely to look again.

There certainly *did* seem to be something constrained in the young lady's attitude. And *that*—was it an effort for freedom?"—a last, all-but powerless endeavor to fly from some shocking utterance or imminent peril! Then he saw Vamper's hand moving over her brow in slow passes; and her form relaxed and sank back as if into soundest slumber.

Captain Hawksley had had too wide an experience of the world not to know the reality of the mesmeric power, and the sinister meaning of the phenomena he had just witnessed

For a moment his heart swelled, his eyes dilated, and he gasped. Then his hand flew to his pistol-pocket. It was empty; the weapon perhaps having fallen out as he ascended the hill. There was no time to look for it now. He vastly preferred fighting by machinery, as being at once more gentlemanly and more deadly; but he could make formidable use of his bare hands when necessity arose. He sprang forward with swift, silent strides over the thick sod, and vaulted heavily in through the open window, alighting just behind Vamper, as the latter bent, gloating.

Captain Hawksley's momentum made it impossible for him to gain instantly a firm footing or strike a decisive blow; and before he could recover himself, Vamper rallied for defence. The two men faced one another with all the wild beast which underlies human nature glaring out of both; but in one it was the mountain panther, in the other the vile hyena. Vamper was no very unequal antagonist, however. Though perfectly capable of shirking any danger which *could* be shirked, he had the courage and alertness of a demon. If Hawksley had entered with deadly weapons, Vamper would have faced him empty handed without flinching—always supposing that there was no hope of escape by supplication and abasement. Chance had brought them together unarmed, and he was prepared to fight it out with cynical vigilance and audacity, confident in his skill as a boxer.

At the first onset Hawksley found his rapid blows turned successively aside, and received in return a swift, stinging, upward stroke which almost carried him off his feet. Then, fairly possessed by fury, he dashed in upon Vamper regardless of injury, drove him bodily into the hall, and grappled him by the throat with both hands. Vamper, game to the last, clutched back with his left hand as best he could, and beat vehemently with his right fist on Hawksley's face, every blow leaving a disfiguring mark. Nevertheless, he would surely have passed out of our story then and there had not Mr. Armstrong reappeared to save him.

The contestants had scarcely heard their host's astounded " Zounds and death, gentlemen, this is disrespectful to my hospitality !" before they found themselves wrenched apart as by a cyclone. The homily went on, he standing between them.

" This house has never been characterized as a lunatic asylum. If gentlemen must quarrel, there is such a thing as the satisfaction customarily recognized."

" I agree with you, sir," replied Captain Hawksley, stepping back to get clear of Roger's peace-preserving grasp, and holding himself with dignity, in spite of his damaged face. He added, " I beg your pardon, sir."

The older man, seeing whither his hasty language tended, looked uncomfortable, and exclaimed : " Oh, I didn't mean to suggest that exactly, either. It isn't every passionate act that calls for the deprivation of life. But fisticuffs, and in the presence of a lady——"

" I regyard *that* matter just as you do, my dear sir," interrupted the captain.

" Then ' let us have peace.' Let us pacificate," proposed Vamper, extending his hand with a grimace.

" I will not disguise the fact that the same world cannot hold us both," replied Hawksley, with folded arms.

" How I shall lament your departure ! When will you suicide ?" sneered Vamper.

Hawksley made no reply. He had determined on a line of action that should be more effectual than any words.

Roger Armstrong looked from one of them to the other, and then in toward the girl, who still remained so strangely motionless. " What does all this mean ?" he demanded in a voice of rising suspicion.

For a few moments nobody answered. His bewilderment was growing strangely pathetic. It seemed as though that sunny, wholesome human world wherein he abode had been at last invaded by a breath, a more than menacing whisper, from some subtler, less palpable condition of being (long enmeshed, unsuspected, with his own), which his nature forbade him to explore.

He moved like one with the dumb ague, and repeated his question in a suppressed voice.

Captain Hawksley loved truth as he loved honor; but to shield a woman's reputation—and that necessity was most intimately brought home to him now. Anything like an accurate explanation would call forth such an outbreak of Armstrong's wrath as would din the story into the ears of all within reach. It would travel from Smiling Susan, already airing her inseparable mirth around a corner, to the whole neighborhood of servants and their employers. Nor would it be possible to confine rumor to the mere facts. Dangers happily, or at least measurably past, would become actual triumphs of evil in the convictions of every gossip. Jessica would be at best an object of most disparaging pity. The thing was not to be borne. Before the inquiry could be a second time repeated, he answered with all rigid assurance, and quite unable to blush through his blood—

"It is a very simple matter, my dear sir. Mr. Vamper and myself regyard one another's political opinions unfavorably. We exchanged views; and somewhat more—as you saw. Miss Armstrong. may have come in during the altercation, and fainted."

"Zounds and death, so she has!" exclaimed the old gentleman, hurrying toward her. Then he turned and rushed to another room for water.

As he passed out Hawksley and Vamper exchanged glances. That of the former spoke deadly menace; that of the latter, satirical defiance. They seemed, however, to agree on one point. In pursuance of that agreement Vamper took one of Jessica's hands in his left, and with his right made certain passes for rousing the mesmeric sleeper. He stopped as her uncle's step approached; but she was already opening her eyes.

"Ah, chafing her hands!" exclaimed Mr. Armstrong;

"that's right, gentlemen. Let me get there to sprinkle her."

But Jessica struggled up to a sitting posture, and put the water aside with her free hand, saying feebly, "Never mind, Uncle, I am better now."

Vamper then released her other hand. Hawksley, watching him, fancied that The Lady's Ring, which she wore thereon, emitted a faint flash or glimmer of light. It was an odd apparition for a sane man to behold, but one who has been vehemently pounded about the optic nerves may see almost anything.

As soon as Mammy Charlotte came on the scene, the captain resigned to her his post beside Jessica, with a word and a glance of warning which were not thrown away. Then he announced that he should leave at once for Nodaway. Mr. Armstrong, finding him resolved, offered to drive him thither, but this was declined, Hawksley wishing to avoid further inquiries.

"It is no fault of mine that you have quarrelled and will not remain," protested his host with a wounded air, as they parted at the gate.

"My dear sir, I know that," answered Hawksley; "I'm coming back when that fellow is out of the way."

"He will go soon," said Mr. Armstrong.

"Can't you induce him to abridge even that?" asked the captain, feeling that he was giving Vamper a last chance.

Roger Armstrong looked puzzled and troubled.

"I have hinted as far as decency would allow. I cannot well do more. Now *can* I?"

"No, sir," assented Hawksley; "but perhaps there may be a providential interposition. Meanwhile, I think it would benefit your neice if you were to take her out for a drive this afternoon. Nothing so good as fresh air, sunlight, and exercise for one who is disposed to be delicate."

CHAPTER XI

Vamper was cordially dissatisfied. Thwarting had followed thwarting, and now his secret was known to at least one man whose very silence was deadly. He must leave the neighborhood, and that soon, or remain forever. Should he leave it, *alone* ?

He thought these things over elaborately, as he sat after dinner under a great drooping willow, near the house, with an eye for every cover whence a rifle ball could come. His view commanded a considerable reach of road, down which Jessica and her uncle were driving. A single approaching horseman passed them with a rather formal salute. Vamper saw the carriage halt soon after and Mr. Armstrong peer out backward, as though half inclined to return. But either his own inertia or his companion's remonstrance overcame this tendency, and they drove on again. Then the watcher's attention was drawn once more to the horseman, who came steadily nearer.

At first Vamper meditated withdrawing to the house, but on seeing that the new comer was small and not very truculent looking, he concluded to stand his ground. The little man dismounted at the gate, and walked jauntily up to him, saying—

"I believe I have not had the honor, sir, of meeting you befo'. Permit me to introduce myself as Lieutenant White, of the Confederate army."

Vamper looked at him with impertinent quizzicalness.

"Jess so—!" said he, drawling; "and yet your colors are hardly subdued enough for that."

The dapper lieutenant, who had rather over attired himself for this interview, flushed angrily, and said—

"I did not come here to qua'll with a Yankee, sir. Captain Hawksley, sir, has seen fit to treat you as a gentleman, sir, and as an equal, sir; and if you'll be kynd enough, sir, to indicate your friend, we will settle this matter befo' long, sir. But your kyard would not be considered by me, sir."

When the little lieutenant's dignity rose in wrath, the "sirs" came as fast as the black motes from a pepper box. Vamper enjoyed the scene hugely.

"Now, you don't say!" he drawled in reply.

"Please name your friend," cried the other, stamping his little foot.

"Friend? friend?" drawled Vamper, as if trying to recall some forgotten term. "Ah, yes. Ahem!—'friend, an extinct species supposed to have passed away with the mastodon and the dodo.' Ahem—dictionary."

"Have you nothing more to the purpose to say than that?" asked the lieutenant, fuming, as he drew an envelope from an inner pocket. "I have come to bring this, in the capacity of Captain Hawksley's friend, and——"

"Are you really a *friend?*—Captain Hawksley's friend?" interrupted Vamper, with the air of one who inquires about a questionable monstrosity.

"I have that honor, sir," replied the lieutenant.

Vamper walked first to the right, then to the left, as if to see all sides of this phenomenon.

"Well, well," commented he, meditatively. "Does he take good care of you? Where does he keep you? Do you think, now, he would sell you out to me at a fair valuation? Perhaps you might get better fodder than he seems to have given you."

The military man flared out at this, "You are a liar, sir," he cried in all his inches.

"Good Lord!" laughed Vamper, mockingly, "Have you just found that out?"

White continued, bewildered by this admission, "And I suspect that you are also a coward, sir."

"Not a doubt of it!" assented Vamper, airily; "likewise a scoundrel and a villain, a four-footed reprobate, and a pattern bed-quilt with the measles. Anything that suits! Let us specify iniquities! Let us catalogue!"

The lieutenant looked at him almost with alarm, saying inwardly, "I don't thank Hawksley for sending me to a lunatic." He thrust the envelope silently into Vamper's hand.

Ishmael raised it to his nose, sniffed at it, and lowered it with a disgusted air. Then he gingerly extracted and read the letter. It concluded as follows:

"No doubt you will consider anything involving personal risk a relick of barbarism not to be countenanced by your example; but perhaps your valour may be stimulated by the assurance that if you do not meet me this afternoon I shall assuredly shoot you down on sight—and that within twenty-four hours.

"I have the honour to be,
　　"Very respectfully,
　　　"Your obedient servant,
　　　　　"ARCHER HAWKSLEY."

It is due to the captain to say that he had never before inserted a threat in a request for "satisfaction." His good taste revolted from anything like compulsion in such matters. But the present document (based on his knowledge of Vamper) was meant rather as a fair warning than as a preliminary to the duello.

Vamper read it through; and then looked up, showing the decorous face of a gentleman with a grievance.

"And you seriously ask me to meet on equal terms an illiterate fellow like that?" he demanded, with a touch of querulous indignation.

"Illiterate!" exclaimed the matter-of-fact lieutenant.

"Yes," pursued Vamper, in the manner of an expounder. "What else can one call a man who spells relic with a *k* and valor with an *u?* Would you have me match my chivalry against a pretender who cannot even spell honor aright?— Perish the base thought!"

The lieutenant saw that he was laughed at; but felt like ending the interview on any terms.

"Then your answer is—'No,'" suggested he, mildly.

Vamper drew himself up with a mock lordly air, and said—"My answer is that whenever Captain Hawksley learns enough about honor or valor to spell it, I will consider any communication which he may make."

Then dropping to the dejected air of one overwhelmed by a sudden revelation of human depravity, he added—

"Lord bless me, the fellow would spell chivalry with an *s!*"

Lieutenant White turned his back on Vamper and walked stiffly away. Ishmael made monkey faces after him for half a minute: then called loudly—"I say!" There was no answer. He called again, "*O* 'oo, White!" Still no answer. Then he shouted suddenly, "There's a wasp on your breeches."

Even military dignity was not proof against this attack. The lieutenant leaped in something very like a panic; and then began a series of twistings, slappings, searchings, and curvetings which infinitely diverted his chief spectator and made all the circus-loving little negroes in the neighborhood yell with delight. At last he stopped, and, looking back at Vamper's solemnly sympathetic face, asked fiercely: "What do you mean?—you *lunatic?*"

Vamper replied, as if calmly summarizing an anecdote— "The moral of which is—'never believe a liar'!"

The lieutenant cast a vindictive and scornful glance behind him, and walked off to his horse.

Not long after he reappeared before his principal, who sat decorously, but with a badly bruised face, in a room of the Nodaway Hotel.

" I wash my hands of the affair," exclaimed White, excitedly. " I never was so bedeviled in my life. On my soul, I
believe you are as crazy as he is. I never heard of such
conduct befo'."

" Take a glass of whiskey to settle your nerves," suggested
Hawksley, calmly, though inwardly he was shaking with natural human amusement over the discomfiture of his friend.

After refreshment, White was able to relate his woes.

" Well, for one thing, he refuses to receive any communication that isn't spelled to suit him. He says you must send
him a letter that spells relic without a _k_. Great Heaven! was
there ever such a reason for declining a challenge ?"

" I'll send him something better than that," answered Hawksley, smiling affably, but with a distortion due to sore muscles.

" You wouldn't shoot a lunatic !" protested White.

" There's more method in his madness than you know of.
May I borrow your horse ?"

" Certainly."

As they were about separating on the outskirts of the village a few minutes later, Hawksley, feeling that he had not
been duly sympathetic, said with friendly concern—

" I am exceedingly sorry that your kind service to me
proved so unpleasant to you."

Then, while listening to the other's polite reassuring phrases,
he incidentally drew his new revolver and examined its loaded
chambers one by one. This shooting at a man, was, after all,
different from target practice. There was far more need to
make no mistakes.

He rode to within half a mile of Jessica's home ; then turned
into a part of the woods, dismounted, removed his saddle and
bridle, and tethered his horse so that the latter could feed comfortably. Secrecy would be of more avail than open approach,
both for guarding Jessica and for his other purpose.

He drew near to the house from a number of points ; under
cover, as if stalking a deer. He saw Jessica and her uncle return from their drive ; he saw them sit down together to their

supper; he saw Mammy Charlotte return from some expedition and go up with Jessica to her room, evidently as a guard; but he did *not* see anything of Ishmael Vamper. He conjectured, rightly, that the latter had left the house and gone into hiding, but this was only a further reason for vigilance.

Captain Hawksley resolved not to relax *his* for a moment. As the darkness settled down, he drew nearer and nearer to the house, pacing about it as noiselessly as the spectral lady of the legend, whom he half fancied at times that he could see in glimpses, down by the leaden gleam of the water. When the moon rose, he took post under the linden tree, where he could watch his lady love's darkened windows, and see that no harm came near her. At dawn he withdrew to the edge of the woods. Then he remembered that it was the day of rest.

The sun rose; breakfast time came and went; the great family carriage was brought round to the steps; Mr. Armstrong and Jessica descended them and entered it; far away a bell was sounding dreamily. "She will be safe in church," thought Hawksley.

The loss of food and sleep had told upon him far more than in his campaigning days. He did not feel quite sure of his aim that morning, and after all he would rather not shoot the fellow on Sunday. It might be a good deed, but he doubted whether it were not breaking the Sabbath. So he saddled his horse and rode sedately back to Nodaway.

CHAPTER XII.

"I CAN CALL SPIRITS."

On Saturday afternoon, after Mammy Charlotte had seen Jessica and Mr. Armstrong drive away, her love had taken counsel of superstition, and the latter sent her to "old Nance" of the Big Cypresses.

The place was enough to raise the spirits of doubt and dread, if no others. A long rib-like bit of land ran down between a narrow inlet, choked with broad-padded water-plants, and the narrow Stygian river. The abnormal and funereal, yet graceful foliage overhead brought about a premature twilight, which had its dismal elements in the shadowy fluted boles, the distorted protuberant knees, the weighted vines and less definable distant shapes. There were no near sounds, except the slow flap of the bittern passing down the stream, the singing and croaking of the frogs which already scented evening, and now and then the startled cry of the black duck, as she rose from the shallow water to escape some fancied danger.

The negress who had wisely made this suggestive spot her home belonged to a class not wholly unknown even in our cities. Like the Norseman of the dark ages, the African-American sometimes worships alternately the new god and the old. However confident he may be of "saving grace," there is always a chance that the next stress of weather will strand him on the hidden and slowly crumbling reefs of fetichism. Possibly he has more excuse therefor than we are willing to allow. We laugh at the priests and victims of "conjure" in their frequently recurring police-court adventures; yet, perhaps, a patient sifting might find in their pretensions and experiences something worthy of study—some hint of strange natural secrets, blundered upon long ago, and traditionally preserved—some indication of real powers which, being very unusual, seem unearthly.

While Charlotte was hovering in the gloom, half minded to return, the old crone whom she had in mind stepped out so swiftly from behind a large tree that she brought a terror with her.

"Te he!" laughed she. "*Afeard*, is ye? 'Feard o' ole Nance! Why chile, *I* won' hurt ye—*S' long 's ye 'have yerself.*"

This qualification did not help Charlotte to rally her wits.

The uncanny thing went on—

"I know'd ye was a comin'; I know'd it sho' 'nuff. Needn't tell me nuffin'. I done got ready fo' ye. See dem conjure roots? Tell me 'bout conjure 't Cypress Beach! Sho' Charlotte!—dere's bigger conjure yere. But ye mus' pay me, honey, y' hear?—old Nance mus' live."

This preliminary settled, the incantations began. Not far behind the pile of conjuring materials, was an artfully located pyre, over which hung a clumsy representative of the traditional witch caldron, with crude yet effective accessories. She lighted the fire, and thereafter followed great parade of marching, chanting, crooning, and ungainly posturing. As the steam rose and thickened, she tossed one after another of her "conjure roots" and magical herbs into the pot, and watched wreath after wreath swell into vague form and float away. At last there came one which resembled a human form. As it mounted and melted, she cried in delight—

"Dar! Dar! He's gone! Bress de Lor'! Ye may go home, Charlotte, soon's ye like. Ye won' fin' *him* dere."

"But won't he come back?" asked Charlotte.

"No, honey, not 'f ye do 's I tell ye. Take dis yar cypress stick an' measure ofe a piece 's long 's Miss Jessie's foot—measure ofe on her foot at daylight, d'ye hear?—an' bury it deep, chile—an' he won't come back no mo' till dat stick's dried up—sho'!"

On returning to Cypress Beach, Mammy Charlotte was not at all surprised to find that Vamper had departed about the time of the mummery under the Big Cypresses. She had no theory in the matter except "conjure"; and perhaps it is hardly necessary to seek for a better. Equally odd coincidences happen every day.

She slept in Jessica's chamber that night; her turbanned presence, dimly realized, making the jaded girl dream on cheerily amid old childish trifles and pleasures. Charlotte had observed her overstrained, sodden, yet alarmingly expectant look before retiring—and had thought of the bitter counsel given by Job's wife. It was the look of a soul beyond dread, as beyond hope; a soul that had neither a life nor a God. But as the old nurse bent over the sleeper in the soft summer dawn, she wept silently, praising Him for sending His angels in the night watches to make her darling's face beautiful again.

Then she bared the soft, shapely, but rather plump foot— still showing on the delicate-veined skin the marks of its evil tryst—and made most devoutly her magical measure; all the time unconscious that from the one root of religion two very different growths were spreading abroad in her soul.

After breakfast (with some sabbatical twinges of conscience) she cut off the marked portion of the stick; but she thought it safer to defer the burial until Jessica had actually set off for church. Her search for a satisfactory spot was not immediately successful. In one spot she found the ground too hard; in another, too liable to tillage; in a third, her proceedings were more open to espial; in a fourth, there was great danger from rooting swine. Thus her quest came to resemble that of Judas Iscariot's soul in the ballad, as it vainly sought a place to cast its grotesque burden, abhorred of all the elements.

At last she strayed off to the woods beyond the road, and

7

bestowed *her* burden beneath the roots of a ragged towering sycamore.   It was a very safe and secret nook; and she felt vastly confident in her newly-acquired supernatural aid.   She argued that there would be no danger in going to her own little church, then just "taking in," to thank the Lord and " shout" mildly.

But Jessica had not gone to Nodaway.   Before riding far, a deadly faintness had come over her.   " Uncle, please drive back," was all that she could say.

He did so, wondering.

" Don't you feel well, my dear?   Shall I remain with you ?" he asked, as they drove up to the steps.

She shook her head (in a strangely mechanical manner which he did not notice), and he helped her into the house.

Then he remembered that he was great in church as well as in State, and that his duties as warden must not be neglected.

" Well, Jessie, if you really don't require my assistance ; but pray be careful, dear——" and he hurried heavily away with an uncertain air.

CHAPTER XIII.

Jessica had sat for some time under the shadow of another will before she had heard the voice or saw the face to which it belonged. Yet she knew, desolately, that they must be very near.

At last Vamper sauntered in and took her hand. Perhaps it was only the pain of his rough grasp, yet The Lady's Ring seemed to burn like hot metal.

"Come, Jessica," said he, in his grotesque way, "let us elope! let us abscond! let us do a little daylight flitting!"

She went with him like one walking in her sleep. At the porch Smiling Susan met them with her everlasting grin. At the gate they passed the bronze funereal countenance of Noah.

Jessica climbed unassisted into the buggy which was waiting there, and Vamper followed lightly. He drove off in a rattling pace, crossing the river at the first ferry, and penetrated the adjoining county of Maryland. He was at no pains to conceal their movements, taking special delight in the thought that he could inflict open shame and poignant distress alike on the man who was seeking his life, and upon him who had twice saved it.

During this strange drive Jessica never spoke nor looked toward him except when compelled by his will. His pleasure in such compulsion was enhanced by the knowledge that her helpless acquiescence covered what would be loathing, if set free. The chief drawback to his enjoyment was the necessity of watching both the road behind and the recalcitrant black horse, to whose services he had helped himself. Thus far the latter had gone off obligingly in a lordly and most rapid stride, but who could tell when the balky demon would take possession of him.

" Our friend, the Keeaptain," suggested Vamper, pleasantly, " is lamenting by this time. Yea, he maketh woe. Poor Keeaptain! But, Jessica, we will good-Samaritanize him ; we will send him a lively darkey for pistol practice, and he can go on spelling his honor with an *u*. Or shall I send him Jessica when her Ishmael wearies of home seclusion and groweth pervasive ? Could she be happy without her Vamper ? Could she joy ? Could her Mammy's ' honey' disport herself ?——Get on, you brute !"

The great black horse, with his ears thrown back and his limbs suddenly petrified, looked as though he would be delighted to return the compliment with well-shod emphasis. Vamper might be pardoned for fancying him possessed by a hostile intelligence, willing to humor his rider just far enough to thwart beyond recovery.

All around them now were evidences of rural thrift—clean fence-rows, perfectly ordered fields, sleek cattle, and shady, antique farmhouses. Just in front, where the road turned, was a plain Quaker meeting-house, which showed the struggle of the preservative instincts of the people against a hundred and fifty not easily baffled years. Its site was still held under the original royal grant, and its worshippers had changed very little since the primitive days of their faith. They were at prayer now, in perfect silence, which perhaps accounted for Negro's suspicion and repugnance. He had rarely travelled in this direction ; and a religion which neither shouted nor chanted may well have seemed to him something abnormal—something not lightly to be approached on a Sunday afternoon.

Vamper grew more and more wrathful. Words, however grossly spiced, had simply no effect. The brute would certainly cause his capture—*his* capture, at a Quaker meeting ! At last, in desperation, he snatched up the whip, and cut fiercely.

Negro stood for an instant quivering in astonishment, then

rallied and sent his heels flying against the dash-board in rapid succession, while Vamper, with preternatural gesticulation and objurgation, laid on the lash harder and harder. Then the horse leaped forward in a run. By this time the noise had drawn several grizzled elders to the door, and one of them received a fair though sufficiently solid projection, Jessica being on the outside as the buggy turned, was shot into his arms in obedience to the law of tangents. Some seconds elapsed before the confusion of disordered feminine belongings and broad-brimmed male demureness was resolved into its proper elements.

Meanwhile Vamper was fully occupied with holding his own seat and avoiding fence posts. Luckily for him the rush did not last. The stationary tendency returned before they had gone a quarter of a mile. Nothing better then occurred to Vamper than to walk back and see whether his captive was too much crippled to be worth further trouble.

It never occurred to him that Jessica could have any voice in the matter; but people *do* change sometimes, and their changes are not always explicable. Perhaps the physical shock of being flung out of a vehicle, had something to do with it, or the unfamiliar surroundings within the quaint, plain building; but, whatever the cause, as the kindly Quaker women, flocking to her aid, bore her within the door, she wept copiously—for the first time since her troubles began. They were delicious tears, for they seemed like a return to human life. One of the Quaker women seated near her considerately whispered, " Thy friend is unhurt." This made little impression on her. A happy hush seemed to deepen and deepen all around, till at last a seer-like old man with white hair rose and pronounced the words, " Whom Christ hath set free." She remembered that the gift of prophecy was one of those claimed by this unworldly sect. She never saw the prophet afterward, and perhaps it was best so. His text had all the value to her of a personal revelation and promise; but the man himself might have proved (on week days) to be some keen-bargaining small farmer, with few sympathies and a niggardly side toward his household.

A minute later Vamper came also. She heard at her ear his mocking whisper, " Let us pray," and shrank aside, withdrawing her hand, which he had tried to take. Both of them glanced at it. The Lady's Ring was gone. Most likely it had been dislodged in the scramble at the door. When he summoned her half aloud—" Come!" she seemed to detect an undertone of hesitancy, of uncertainty, in his voice, as if he felt that his power over her had slipped from him. Yet the trinket, with all its rarity and strangeness, could hardly have been to him what it was to her—a mystic, wonder-working legacy of long-buried evil—a symbol so charged with the tragic thrill, the stifled passion, and spell-bound despair of an elder day, that it might even yet burn its way into the human heart and will.

Whatever the cause, Jessica felt him waver, and found strength to command in a whisper—" Leave me, or I will denounce you—instantly!"

Vamper, too shrewd to lose his chance of escape, walked to the door, with a very clear sense of failure. No time for meditation was left him; already a well-known horse and rider were in sight. Many a man of less courage, well armed, and wrathful as he was, would have turned at bay; but the impulse to do so passed almost instantly from his mind, the pleasure of killing Hawksley being outweighed by the certainty of some physical damage to himself. The calculation was rapid, but conclusive.

"Art is long, and time is fleeting," he philosophized. " ' I am not what I was, my visions flit.' Let us decamp."

Thereupon he slipped quietly round the building, and dashed for the woods at an astonishing rate. Early the next morning he was seen aboard a train of cars hurrying northward.

CHAPTER XIV.

"WHERE ARE YOU GOING, MY PRETTY MAID?"

After Vamper left her, Jessica sank forward with her face between her hands, and remained so for some little time, no one speaking to her. Most likely the Quaker matrons and maidens, in accordance with their beautiful belief, thought her agitation due to the silent workings of "the spirit." How far were they wrong? She was looking backward into a black pit; then forward into the life and light of freedom.

A slight rustle showed that the meeting was breaking up. She rose and passed out decorously with the rest. As she reached the door, Captain Hawksley rode up, leading back the horse and buggy which Vamper had carried off from Cypress Beach. She noticed that he looked with keen scrutiny from face to face of the sober crowd about her. Then his expression changed, and he raised his hat and said—

"Miss Armstrong, your uncle desires your presence as soon as possible after the service. He is not well. So you have discyarded your escort. Well, I will take his place, with your permission."

As they drove back toward Cypress Beach, he conversed on every conceivable topic except certain recent events and their probable consequences. This studious reticence, however, quite failed to please Jessica. She fancied something almost ostentatious in his elaborate make-believe—and the more so because something within her soul tended frankly and strongly toward him. A little plain speaking on his part would have been a luxury, even if overblunt and not really

more kindly. She seemed to find in every guarded common-
place a distinct reminder of what he did *not* say.

As they reached a branch road turning toward the river, a
steamboat whistled up the stream. She grasped the captain's
arm, with a sudden wild wish, asking, "What is that?" as he
reined in the horse at her bidding.

"That is the *Pocomoke*," he answered, "I understand that
certain parties have run a Sunday excursion from Baltimore.
It is a detestable innovation."

"Oh!" she cried, half rising, with a sudden flash in cheeks
and eyes. "*Won't* you put me on board?"

He began to expostulate. "Miss Armstrong, your uncle——"

"Oh! I can't face him, indeed I can't! Don't you *see* I
can't?" she cried, almost in a terrified tone, covering her face
with her hands.

Then he spoke out manfully after his peculiar fashion, but
at all events with no pretence, good or bad.

"If Mr. Armstrong should disown you, Miss Armstrong,
or even show you unkyindness, I should regyard myself as
called upon to prove to him that there is one who will vindi-
cate you by all methods usual among gentlemen."

"Oh no, it's not *that*," she exclaimed, dropping her hands,
and looking quickly up at him. Then her eyes drooped.
"Do you think I have no sense of shame?" she asked, with
quiet sadness.

He saw that remonstrance was useless. "I will go with
you to Washington," said he.

"You are very kind," she began, with doubt, if not denial,
in her voice.

Hawksley interrupted her with unusual brusqueness. "Suppose *he* should re-appear at one of the lower landings?"

She drew a labored shuddering breath, and replied: "You
are right. I trust all to your vigilance and judgment."

Her tone, even more than her words, brought a pleased
look to his face. She had no inclination to conceal her very

great gratitude for the knightly confiding faith which would not lower itself to doubt or esteem her less precious for all that made against her. There was something very restful in this polished marble pillar of a man—twisted, it may be, into foolscaps and gargoyles in the remoter corners, but withal a thing for weak arms to cling to.

When she found herself quite safe with him upon the boat (the horses and vehicle having been sent back by a safe messenger), and rapidly leaving behind the scene of her humiliation and peril, her native mirthfulness returned, exaggerated a little by the vibration of nerves just relieved from most abnormal tension. She made free with topics which both her heart and head told her were no fit subjects for laughter; even jesting about her good uncle's astonishment when he should get her letter informing him of her whereabouts.

"It will be sorry business for me," answered the captain, a little shocked, but doing his best to fall in with her mood. "No doubt he and everybody will regyard me as the sole culprit, the great original eloper. Miss Armstrong, you have destroyed my reputation."

The captain was not often fortunate in his jocularity. This time the words were hardly out of his mouth before he felt their sinister import, and emphasized it by *showing* that he felt it. A dark vision seemed to pass momentarily before Jessica's face, and she glanced at the finger which yet bore the faint impress of the ring.

Hawksley's wrath passed readily (as it was prone to do) from himself to a more hateful offender. He muttered moodily—

"I should like to have that fellow for a field hand on a good out-of-the-way plantation."

Jessica caught his words. Looking out over the sunset-gloried waters, she exclaimed—

"Pray don't let me hear any more about slavery. It is gone, gone, gone!"

There was an exultation in the last word (she was thinking chiefly of herself) which made him open his eyes and doubt his ears.

"Miss Armstrong," he began, didactically, "slavery——"

She turned toward him with her old childish imperativeness, and laid her hand caressingly on his arm, saying—

"There, there, captain, I've *heard* all those praises."

She threw her head back and laughed softly but merrily at his discomfiture and bewilderment; then stopped and said, musically, with her head held archly aslant, "Jessica will have none of them."

The captain was too pleased by this revival of her kitten-like playfulness and waywardness, even to seem vexed at her singular change of views.

After that they sat on the deck in the twilight and the starlight, while the neighboring groups of rather over-gay excursionists gradually settled into something less noisy under the influence of the hour and the scene. Jessica looked with friendly interest at the flirting city lads and lasses of the plainer sort, the tired artizans and their wives taking a very thorough rest, the sick children already brightened into convalescence by a few ungodly whiffs of salt air and sabbath-breaking.

Her companion could not quite sympathize with this feeling. Such practices were quite contrary to *his* Christianity, and such surroundings were never welcome. In the present instance he certainly had some just grounds for dissatisfaction. How *could* he prosecute his suit (though with everything else tantalizingly in his favor), when on his right hand, not far away, an impassioned dry-goods clerk was whispering out his soul to his shop-tending dulcinea, while on the left a Teutonic grocer was making beery gestures in the direction of his heart? Captain Hawksley hardly knew what to do with his chivalric devotion; and wisely concluded to keep it out of range of ridicule.

However thwarted, he found it very pleasant to be her sole protector, to talk with her hour by hour in the early night, and to draw assurance from her demeanor, her tones, even her playful-earnest rebuke, that he had really awakened some interest in her heart. Long after she had gone below, he sat there thinking over these things alone. He would have been even better pleased if she had not shown such a sudden spirit of revolt against some of the good old traditions. But he set this down to some faint, lingering influence of Vamper; a slightly derogatory breath-film on the glass, soon to pass away.

CHAPTER XV.

"SWEET DAY—SO CALM, SO BRIGHT."

Even in our young country almost every city can show its imperfectly assimilated fragments of an earlier era. To call them antique would sound a little absurd, but they are often at least sufficiently out of fashion to seem out of our modern world also.

Thus going southward from the Capitol, past the massive undermined walls of Duddington Manor and the sarcophagi of masonry over the old Carroll springs—haunted in summer evenings by dusky loiterers and water drawers, with ancestral reminiscences of the desert in the poise of their head-borne burdens—you may chance to find yourself in the Washington of Jefferson's time. For two or three squares nothing is recent. You note the pillared frame buildings with their low porch roofs and patches of yellow moss; the broad, heavy fronts of the brick houses with knockers on the doors which are *not* restorations or imitations; the quaint outlines of mullioned window and sill; the pump standing artlessly here and there; the great width of sidewalk, with its double row of shade-trees.

One of these commodious, though unpretending, old houses had been Jessica's home during many happy seasons and some sorrowful ones indeed she could remember no other. She returned to it—still her property—with a quiet sense of comfort and rejoicing, like a frightened and weary child burying her face in her mother's lap.

She found it right pleasant to be greeted by the familiar sights and sounds, and yet this very sameness made them seem almost unreal. Stranger still was the garrulous questioning of the servants as to what had brought her back *so soon*. Between the incidents of her hopeful departure and the present there stretched an interminable perspective, of a kind which even Memory fled from with shut eyes. How could she measure days with them?

The negroes, with loyal quickness of apprehension, saw that something was wrong, and turned to more serviceable proceedings. They did not for a moment suspect anything discreditable to herself; but said among themselves that she had doubtless had some disagreement (not pleasant to explain) with her kin beyond the bay.

Her neighbors were not at all troublesome, for she had never made many friends in that quiet part of the city; and their conjectures as to her plans and prospects had a comfortable midsummer languor. The sleepy air about her scarcely gave even the faintest rustle of awakening gossip; so that she often seemed to *feel* the mantle of silence which had fallen about her like the invisible veils of Eastern story. Once she found herself dreamily wondering whether the old-time Lady of the Ring were more secluded from the world she had left.

Meanwhile Captain Hawkesly was troubled by the thought that he was suppressing what her uncle ought to know. Almost every day, for he never left her long unguarded, he besought her to write or let him write, but somehow nothing came of it. In truth, she could not keep quite beyond her mental reach the knowledge that all Accomac was alive with flashes of ire and blasts of blame. Here in this little haven she could rock serenely, resting her still quavering nerves amid placid surroundings. She could not let in all that turmoil just yet—no, not even to relieve her uncle's unquestionable distress. But this last thought always transferred a portion of the distress to herself.

This delay made life very pleasant for the captain. With all his honorable tribulation, he would have been more than human if he had not at heart rejoiced at being secluded with the woman he loved. There was a power not to be gainsaid in the light touch of her hand, and the gentle, half-playful shake of her head while she asserted in the most winning of childlike tones Jessica's right to regulate her own affairs. Sometimes she would baffle his advances with sly coquetry and demurely fail to understand them; yet at others she would reveal accidentally (at least it seemed so) her sense that they were likely to have a future in common.

They lived much in the open air at this time, avoiding, however, all spots where acquaintances, with their surprises and surmises, might probably lie in wait. Many of their hours were spent upon the Anacostia River where they were effectually hidden from the more fashionable part of the city, or in rambling through its bordering woodlands. Often, too, they explored the quaint nooks near her home in the pleasant time after sunset when people come out to sit before their houses and old cronies do their gossiping. It was even more charming to lean over the bridge and watch the struggling water ebb away from the piers and spread slowly with a saffron-tinted gleam into the last rays of the sun. But nothing was so delightful as to sit side by side in the old parlor, after one of their excursions, arranging Jessica's floral spoils, and sometimes forgetting all about them in more engrossing converse.

Captain Hawksley could not sufficiently admire Jessica's variety of moods. In proportion as she lost sight of recent distressing events and blossomed into her own bright self again, every phase grew richer and more vivid. Now it was the laughing, butterfly-chasing child, a very romp but for her exquisite grace; now the maiden, listening and trustful, mingling half-awakened affection with virgin reserve; now the mature woman, considering, weighing, discussing, deferent to his greater experience, yet tempering with good sense his more fantastic hopes; now the pitying angel who bent in spirit over all the suffering and oppressed, and refused to believe in any past cruelty or undue sternness of his own. At first he chafed a little at some of these latter sentiments; but she tempered them with such flattering warmth and gentleness that he felt himself greatly blessed to be allowed to love her more and more. All in all, this dream-courtship by the Anacostia was an episode not to be looked back upon without that feeling of mingled sadness and sweetness which attends the death of a midsummer day.

But Jessica was not in all respects precisely the same Jessica as of old. She had lost almost wholly her over-estimate of the merely artificial part of life. She had gained an aversion, which was *more* than aversion to all false shows and hollowness. A sense of the hideousness of oppression and of moral evil seemed to have been branded, as by hot iron, into her soul.

These changes might be only temporary, but there were some others which *must* be so—or there would be danger in them. Now and then a sudden silence would come over her like a shadowy wing. Sometimes, at a chance allusion, or even when no one spoke, she would start with a look of agony and appeal, or a furtive, shivering glance into empty air. Then out of its decorously curtained niches in the deeper shadows of Captain Hawksley's soul would stalk a figure which Ishmael Vamper would do well to shun. Indeed, to do him justice, he *would* have shunned it had he once looked into that heart as we look into it now. He could not then have been bribed to visit Cypress Beach by a world full of piquant possibilities. He held the keys to many unamiable endowments, such as malignity for the pleasure of malignity, vengeance for the enjoyment of vengeance, the love of wreck and ruin for the rare delight in them; but neither the logical nor the fantastic elements of his mind enabled him to conceive of a set destructive purpose unconnected with any idea of gratification, at once a fanaticism and a duty, unappeasable, immitigable, inevitable— grim as a law of nature.

One day Jessica and Captain Hawksley were returning from a boating excursion; he at the oars, she seated in the stern. The sun, sinking behind the city, threw the nearer buildings into irregular prominence, and sprinkled bits of incandescent metal on the house fronts of the opposite bank. Their voices grew quieter in the settling hush of twilight; then ceased altogether. Jessica's eyes sought the marvellous beauty of the west in yearning and adoration. Hawksley's face seemed to have caught the same expression, reflected, as he gazed upon her.

"Jessie," said he, his voice hardly rising above a whisper in the stillness, and the oars trailing idly.

She had never heard him address her in that way before, and there was a little gleam of surprise in her face as it turned toward his—thoughtfully, steadily; but the tenderness was there still.

"Jessie," he repeated gently and slowly, with a slight thrill in his voice, "the day is passing and our lives are passing likewise." He paused, as if tremulous; yet less in real doubt of her answer to what he was about to say than a hovering expectancy tinged with joy too great to be real. She, waiting with no aspect of denial, leaned a little aside, one hand rippling the water. But possibly under that calm surface an even fainter ripple of sinister association, or some equally impalpable influence, was making itself felt.

However that may be, there came a sudden change. Her hand left the water and clutched the gunwale to aid her in rising, and she shuddered toward him, speechless like an embodiment of horror. Every line of face and figure expressed a strangled shriek. She was saved from falling overboard only by his arm lightly thrown round her.

This touch seemed to cause an awakening; for her face grew at once more natural and she withdrew to her seat, still trembling violently and compelling a laugh. Hawksley asked no questions, but the last reflected glint of sunset striking his eyes made them like a panther's by torchlight.

Before long she reverted to the subject, explaining nervously, "There is so much one can't account for. You know what people say when you shiver?—I think some one must have been walking over the grave of my soul that time."

"My dear Miss Armstrong," exclaimed Hawksley, horror-stricken, "pray dismiss such ghastly fancies. They will do you no good."

"Good!" she laughed, bitterly; then, suddenly changing as she pointed to the wharf, she exclaimed in delight, "Mammy Charlotte! Oh, do make haste!"

As the oars urged them landward, she settled down cosily, purring "Dear Mammee," with an affectionate dwelling on the vowels and multiplication of syllables.

As the boat grazed the wharf she sprang lightly ashore. and seized and wrung both of Charlotte's brown-yellow hands. "Oh you are as good as gold," she cried; "Jessica says so."

Mammy Charlotte's response was tempered with a certain reproachful gravity.

"Bress de Lor', Miss Jessie, I *know'd* I'd find you here. Marse Roger, he wouldn' pay no 'tention. 'No, Charlotte,' he says, 'I know she couldn' go to leave me dat way.' 'She's dead; Jessica's dead,' he keeps a sayin'. Fus' he ramped, an' he subtended de whole neighborhood; an' now he seems to 'a' los' all his enermation. He jess sits an' looks like he didn' know nothin'. Oh, Miss Jessie, honey, how *could* ye go to do it?"

Here Captain Hawksley, coming within range, was favored with her nearest possible approach to a vindictive scowl. Without waiting for an answer, she turned her batteries obliquely on him.

"Yes, Miss Jessie, Marse Roger hasn' heer'd one single word from ye, an' he keeps a sayin': 'Dat vampire an' dat gorilla have made away wid her atween 'em.' Dat's wat he keeps a sayin', Miss Jessie."

8

"Hush-h!" said Jessica, in a distressed tone. Then, seeing that this failed measurably in its effect, she added, drawing up a little, "If he really thought so, would he be sitting still at Cypress Beach? Now, now, I really can't have this, Charlotte."

"I dunno, Miss Jessie," began Charlotte, in reply to the young mistress's first sentence, with the respectful yet dogmatic obstinacy of her race and station.

But Jessica interrupted her with "There, there, don't scold, Tell me something nice. I know you must have some pleasant news, Mammy."

There was something almost comically wheedling in her affectionate tone. Charlotte's features condescended to relax; but before she spoke the captain suggested—

"Well, Miss Armstrong, as you will be safely gyarded home, and will no doubt have much to say to our good friend here, perhaps——"

He halted irresolutely; but Jessica's indecision did not tempt him to continue with her. Indeed, she was for the moment too much engrossed with affairs in Accomac to think of anything else. So he merely added, "Good-bye," and raised his hat, turning away with a rather bitter sense of the world's injustice. So Mr. Armstrong had at last concluded him to be "a guerrilla!" Once upon a time his patriotic services had been honored with a different title. What galled him worst of all was that he could not feel wholly free from blame. He had allowed himself to drift into a false position, and must accept the consequences.

His preoccupation did not prevent him from hearing Jessica utter a low, breathless exclamation. Involuntarily he slackened his pace and listened. The two whom he had left were hardly within earshot; but Mammy Charlotte in her earnestness had raised her voice so that he distinguished the words—"Yes, I seen him over yere a lookin' out on de water: an' you were dere, Miss Jessie. O do be moughty keerful."

Captain Hawksley could not doubt to whom these words referred, and they tallied strangely with Jessica's agitation in the boat. He wondered if it could be more than a coincidence. He tried to quiet himself with the suggestion that the old mulatto might have mistaken her man. But the thought so weighed on his mind, that at last he wheeled about and marched with a forbidding brow to the spot which she had indicated. One or two loungers of whom he made inquiry seemed in doubt as to whether they had or had not seen a person answering to his description of Vamper. They showed, however, an amiable willingness to suppose they had seen him if this supposition would do their questioner any good. It was plain that he could learn nothing reliable.

Nevertheless the possibilities thus suggested, as well as everything which had happened since sunset, left a residuum of gloom in his mind which harmonized well with the darkness deepening round him. Stern doubts and dire anxieties made themselves felt as he stood gazing over the glimmering waters; but it was not in them to turn him from his course. When he had faced them all down unflinching, he turned with a loyal resolve that, come good or come evil, Jessica should have the protection of his hand and his name against all manner of harm; that is, if she *would* have it, for he did not feel altogether confident.

This time he was admitted by Mammy Charlotte; the kindness of whose manner showed that Jessica's explanation had done him full justice. He knew that her influence, notwithstanding, was likely to be adverse; but he was very willing to conciliate, so far as he knew how.

"Your coming was a surprise to us, Charlotte," he said, with a slight tone of patronage; "but it shows a fidelity which no friend of Miss Armstrong can fail to appreciate. I regyard it as very creditable to you. It will be easy to set matters right now."

Charlotte shook her head—

"Mighty hard, sir, I'm afeard, mighty hard!" Then she added, conscientiously, "If Miss Jessie'd only took your advice, sir, about writin'!"

As she spoke, she ushered him into the parlor, and went after her young mistress. Presently Jessica entered and walked straight up to him, graceful as ever, but with no buoyancy.

"You seem weary," he said, taking her hand, "and saddened," he continued, as they seated themselves on the sofa.

"How can I help it?" she asked, sorrowfully. "Do you not see what I have done? The trouble, the shame, the distress! If I had listened to you! If I had only done as you advised about returning to Cypress Beach!"

He pressed her hand respectfully, and replied with persuasive firmness—

"Then listen to me now, Miss Armstrong. If you have learned to regyard me as a safe gyide in this instance try me permanently. I shall not fail you. I am not uttering the sentimentalities which boys offer to gyurls, but you know well my affection—and—you love me, Jessie, is it not so?"

She answered, gently, "Yes," but there was little encouragement in the word.

He looked puzzled and baffled, but came to the point with the inquiry—

"May I consider myself accepted?"

She hesitated, struggling inwardly between the temptation to take the easy and pleasant path of assent, and the urgent need to stop short and utter what was on her conscience, however distressing the topic. Mammy Charlotte's return from Cypress Beach had compelled Jessica to open her eyes suddenly and very widely indeed on some things that she had been striving to ignore. At last she raised her face, pale but resolute, and began to speak in an enforced, steady voice. But before long the stir of feeling broke through her self-imposed calm.

"It is not possible," she said, "that you have duly considered what you ask for, Captain Hawksley. How can I be mean enough to take you at your word, when you do not foresee what it involves? What man of your proud temperament would wish for a wife of whom every gossip will be saying—what—you well know—if you think a moment—they are saying against *me?* Worst of all, about whom so much that is humiliating may *truly* be said! O God and Father above, how can You permit such things?"

"What!" he cried, starting in horror at a suspicion which now for the first time stirred his mind.

She read it as clearly as if written, and, conquering her passionate outburst, replied with quiet bitterness—

"Oh, you know the worst. What mercy is in salvation at the eleventh hour—*that* I have experienced. But is it nothing to feel that one's heart and soul and will have been desecrated and bemired by that—that creature's—infernal power? that even his loathsome kisses——" she half drew back her her hand, looking at it with abhorrence, and shuddering almost as she had shuddered in the boat.

"That is enough!" answered Hawksley, with stern emphasis. "That lies between him and me. Now as you obeyed him through compulsion, obey me through love. Never let that subject be mentioned again between us."

Jessica answered very humbly and thankfully—

"It shall be as you wish."

"In all respects?"

She nodded.

"Then I may bring the ring to-morrow?"

"Would you not like to see my uncle first?" with reviving archness.

He stifled an exclamation under the merry reproof of her look; and answered chiefly by a kiss that sent the roses into her cheeks. But as he was departing, an hour later, he felt called upon to reply in words, with his most deferential manner—

"Of course, miss Armstrong, your uncle shall be apprised without delay of our betrothal, subject to his consent."

She bowed decorously, but with a little demurely mischievous sense of humor in so much elaboration of ceremony after such intimate endearments. Her amusement took another turn, when, turning her eyes from the closing door, she saw Mammy Charlotte pass in another direction shaking her head with an expression of dire misgiving. A certain amount of discontent might of course be looked for, and Jessica knew her retainer's time-honored way of manufacturing omens to suit any unwelcome occasion; so the young lady merely drew her arm-chair to an open window, and, in defiance of all prognostics, set about being sedately happy.

More than once before, Jessica had watched the winking stars in this way, and woven her plans for the future; but she assured herself that there was a radical difference between then and now. Obviously she was not in a flirtation or a love affair, but in love. The whole current of her being was set in one direction, drawn by the powerful personality of her betrothed. In spite of some acknowledged foibles, he seemed to her the very man of men. She insisted strenuously that she never could be happy without him. She doubted her worthiness to be his wife; but vowed that she would at least prove a devoted one. In a word, that evening's event, with its extrication from all difficulties, and assurance of his congenial lifelong company and protection, filled her soul with a joyous glow which even an expert might well mistake for an undying affection.

CHAPTER XVI.

"OVER THE MOUNTAINS OF THE MOON."

While Jessica built castles in the air, her husband-elect was walking in rather stately meditation toward the heart of the city. By all rules, his face ought to have illuminated the darkness; but it did not. He was ill at ease in his victory. An ominous sensation, almost amounting to a distinctly outlined fancy, haunted his mind, that something had happened, or was about to happen, which would make strongly against his hopes. It may have been no more than a revulsion from his recent ecstatic delight; but it gained upon him more and more, until it seemed to urge him from the thoroughfare which he had thus far followed, out across a dreary waste of sparsely settled commons which stretched to the westward.

The moon rose as he went on, and made that unkempt region look stranger than ever. Away to the right towered airily the pale pillared wings and swelling dome of the Capitol. Far to the left a shadowy clump of foliage marked the Arsenal grounds. Just before him a broad arch of masonry spanned a stream which issued at this point into an open channel. Two or three skeleton-masted sloops were moored to the bank not far below, but they did not look as if meant for any earthly use or service. He walked to the edge of the archway and peered down in silence. A bat or two passed in beneath him to unknown depths. All that he could see was cavernous, black, suggestive of every foulness. He remembered Coleridge's "through darksome caverns fathomless to

man down to a sunless sea;" but it seemed a shame to link
anything poetical even in thought with what was so noisome.

Hawksley drew back, and was about to resume his walk,
when a succession of yells from the direction of the Arsenal—
distant, but coming nearer and nearer—made him halt and
listen. He had no difficulty in conjecturing their cause.
Even his recent complete absorption in the dream-world
of his dearest emotional interest, had not quite closed his
eyes and ears to the greater and more stirring life outside.
In favor of Jessica and her image, he had temporarily abdi-
cated his post as political observer, critic, and prophet; but in
those days there were some things which would force themselves on one's notice even when not observant. He knew
that the contagion of disorder had spread from city to city
until men everywhere dreaded or hoped for a general labor
insurrection. Every day brought its reports of tumultuous
mobs, interrupted communications and destruction of property—and the tide was still rising.

Even at the capital, with the least possible material to work
upon, the spirit of discord made itself felt. For some time in
the busier parts of the city there had been considerable
activity among that class of strikers whose self-assertion
freely takes the form of preventing other men from working.
Of late, an astute leader had introduced new and sinister
tactics, gathering the previously scattered and casual bands
into a single permanent body, which paraded the streets under
his leadership by day, and bivouacked on the commons at
night. The menace of their presence was enough to extort
supplies of all kinds from the more timid shopkeepers; so the
strength and boastfulness of the party were growing daily.
Some said the same of their leader's designs; but as yet he
had attempted nothing very audacious. He passed for the
most part under a disreputable nickname, which may have
been chosen to flout and bemock the decency of the community: so that Hawksley, not actually meeting him, had
never thought of him as Ishmael Vamper. But now the old

nurse's narration came into the captain's mind, as well as a certain parallelism of traits and conduct; so he decided grimly enough, that it was best to wait. Perhaps he might be providentially enabled to kill his enemy without breaking even a moral law.

Presently he heard the shouts and cries again, but in more angry tones, and dim figures came into view. Next there were pistol-shots in rapid succession and other sounds of fight. Then a knot of men appeared, scattering as they ran toward him, pursued by a much larger body. One or two of the fugitives passed close by the immovable captain, as he stood, revolver in hand, searching the faces behind—which now halted irresolutely—for the only one which he earnestly wished to spoil by a bullet. Most of those faces were of a dirty bronze or bilious yellow, even by moonlight, and did not ruffle his stern vigilant scorn; but his eyes opened in almost incredulous amazement and abhorrence as he saw among them the fine, clear features of his recent associate, Robert Chauncey. Very reckless features they certainly were just then, with some inner exaltation of feeling lighting up that recklessness, and a sharp personal enmity dashed through it. A better light might have showed a suspicious flush in his cheeks; but as it was you could plainly see a revolutionary disorder of costume and manner which was more significant than any flush. He was not very far out of harmony with his surroundings after all.

CHAPTER XVII.

"AND THEN HE FALLS."

In truth fortune had used Robert Chauncey very ill. He had returned to the city crestfallen and bitterly jealous, but with a determination to do something—he knew not what—something to dazzle and win Jessica—something signally heroic, romantic, noble. But one disappointment had followed another, and turned all good intentions sadly awry. The clerkship under Government so long filled by him faithfully and well (all the better, perhaps, because of his easy, undistracted temper) had already melted away from him with most astounding facility. During his very brief and fully authorized absence, a dependent nephew of a great senator and capitalist had been quietly and respectably provided for to the satisfaction of all parties, except the one who was dispossessed. *He* was naturally biassed against the change: and indeed declared almost offensively that it was outrageous to discharge an official merely because he had no uncle who was a legislative railway magnate.

This outburst of indignation no doubt consoled and relieved him in some degree; but its value was wholly subjective. The chief of his bureau merely expressed his regret that everybody could not be retained forever; adding, more graciously, that for his own part he would bear willing testimony to Mr. Chauncey's competency, urbanity and fidelity, in case the latter should care to apply for reinstatement to the head of the Department, with whom of course the decision of the matter would rest. His own recommendation, however, was to treat the occurrence as a blessing in disguise, and not to give up for a paltry regular stipend all the unlimited opportunities open to a young man in our growing country. Here he smiled with an air of self-satisfied and encouraging wisdom; but (as Chauncey discovered not long afterward without surprise) his very next act was to send a brief note to the powers above announcing the probable visit of the discharged man, and requesting refusal. Then, with a truly official stomach and digestion, he walked to a neighboring restaurant to lunch more elaborately than usual (by the aid of a very recent windfall); and as he returned serenely, he paused at a broker's office for a dignified inspection of the gold and stock tape.

But the case had a side which was not at all humorous to the young man who thus beheld his livelihood and defined position in this artificial world gliding away after his dearest love-prospects like the withdrawn scenes of a panorama. The magical ease with which such assured and habitual things had been transmuted into bodiless and elusive vapor, made it all seem very unreal. He had at first a curious sensation of drifting at the sport of something which would make very light of any will, and of wondering where it would bear him next. He was rather in the half-amused attitude of a critical, unconcerned passenger than that of the man at the helm. But this could not last. No self-delusion could make the loss other than serious, even distressing.

To duly understand this, one must take the standpoint of the Government clerk who has acquired by lapse of time a placid, nebulous sense of permanency, and also of unfitness for other pursuits. Robert Chauncey had a sort of half-formulated idea (which he would have ridiculed if crudely stated) that his office belonged to him; so that the actual wrong which he had sustained grew prodigiously in his fancy.

Moreover, like most of his tribe, he had made no provision for the inevitable, but had lived from month to month as if there were never to be a change. All of his available funds

had been spent during his recent excursion across the Chesapeake, and his tailor had seemed to divine the precarious state
of his affairs almost before it existed. His pocket pleaded
pathetically for supplies, but whither could he turn for them?
His friends condoled with him and offered good advice, which
lacked nothing except availability. Much of it related to
using his artistic talents, so that he grew presently to hate
the word "art." He could do fifty things pretty cleverly, but
now that the pinch had come they all somehow seemed to be
things which no o e was willing to pay for. His efforts to
secure reinstatement or appointment to another Government
office were foredoomed to failure. Indeed, under existing
institutions and doctrines, there was no valid reason why he
should be appointed. With all his easy-going politeness and
ready deference, he had never fawned or truckled, nor in his
seclusion from politics had he acquired the means of repaying
patronage by partizanship; so he could not rely on the advo-
cacy of any one of the little great men of the day.

As for any private employment offering light duties such as
he had been accustomed to, or even those heavier ones from
which the delicately nurtured theoretical democrat recoils
more promptly than even the avowed aristocrat—the market
was overstocked. He had hardly formed in his own mind the
half-ironical petition for work, when it was thrown back at
him—the direst of echoes—from every quarter of the land.
"Work! work! work!" the cry went up; "Give us work at
living wages!" and the fearful emphasis of bloody acts was
laid again and again upon the ominous words.

He was in no condition to analyse or discriminate. Their
cry was his cry; their wrongs were his wrongs; their foe was
his foe. Hitherto his sentimental socialism had been much
like that of the French nobles who adored Rousseau, and dis-
creetly ran away from Marat and his guillotine. But now,
having after all no insuperable barriers of class or fortune between him and the insurgents, this sympathy became a living
force. Every chord in his kindly and justice-loving nature

was stirred by the recital of manufacturers' oppressive treatment of their "hands," the heartlessness and cruelty shown
by great corporations, and, in short, the great array of
wrongs which poverty and weakness have always suffered at
the will of those above them. He had leisure enough and
to spare for tuch tales now, and many of them, true and false
together, naturally flowed into his ears. Hitherto he had
been rather favorably disposed toward uniforms and their
wearers, who undoubtedly numbered some very creditable
dancers and small-talkers; but now he found himself in a
mildly virulent way passing satirical comments on the Government of a free country which would turn its hired bayonets over to the service of a plutocracy. He took to haunt-
ing divers suburban. resorts where the beer was better than
the political economy, and exchanging significant jests and
wishes with the idle and reckless fellows who gathered there.
Sometimes these innuendoes related to what might be done
without going very far from home—idle, foolish vaporing (for
the most part) of those who had nothing at stake and would.
not really incur any personal risk!

But in Robert Chauncey's mind something more like a
serious purpose was gradually taking shape. Through all
his other troubles he still felt the sting of Jessica's contempt;
and he seemed to see it reflected in the face of every young
lady on whom he called—for to the last he kept up this
habit. When a man has an assured income behind him, he
may safely call himself a trifler with an airy grace; but it
is no joke to be called so or thought so by others, when he is
out of heart and cash and credit. His charming partners
were as gracious as ever, but he began to fear that they did
not respect him very highly after all; and he found this more
galling than would have seemed possible a few weeks before.
He felt that the only conceivable way of setting himself right,
even in his own eyes, was by proving that he had forceful and
daring traits. This might not win Jessica, who was sure to

be on the conservative side, but it would compel her attention and regard.

On the evening of Mammy Charlotte's return he strolled away from one of the threatful suburban gatherings before mentioned with more than usual bitterness in his soul. An hour or two before he had heard with seemingly placid surprise the undoubted fact of Jessica's elopement with Captain Hawksley, as related by a dear feminine friend, who began in solemn horror, and ended giggling. As a result his words had been less guarded than usual, and he had given himself free rein in other ways. The blood was hot and wrathful about his brain, and every element of his nature, good or bad, conspired to make him absurdly ripe for mischief.

As he moved along, a tumult of steps came up behind, an arm was passed familiarly through his own, and he found himself marching at the head of a tattered procession. He made an angry motion to disengage himself, when Vamper's voice suggested quizzically, " Let's get an office."

Chauncey was in too misty a mood to recall either past experiences or old maxims. Glass houses were no more to him than the discarded civilities which he so long had worshipped. He felt the need of a little incongruous objurgation—if only for its bizarre novelty and freedom—so, with a declamatory flourish of arms and voice, he shouted, " To the devil with offices and office-holders—Robbers of the people !"

This, his first speech in public, was greeted with tumultuous approval. Thereupon Vamper turned and waved his hand backward with mock grace, saying, "*Behold* the people."

Robert Chauncey beheld, but not clearly enough to take Vamper's real meaning. The only face which impressed him— like a gargoyle—was that of Mammy Charlotte's son John, who had followed her or Vamper to a place which could well have spared him ; and even in its distorted savagery, as in the vaguer scarecrow array trooping behind, the young enthusiast, doubly intoxicated by wine and philanthropy, could see nothing but the pitiable effects of long-continued, degrading oppression. He called aloud, "Oh that I could strike one good blow in your cause, men and brethren!"

"Certainly, strike! We *are* strikers," commented Vamper, encouragingly, and with huge enjoyment. John merely whooped.

By this time the behavior of his companions—or was it only the cool night air—began to make Robert Chauncey less exuberant in utterance; but his enthusiasm still ran high. He felt that he was going to do battle with those who grind the faces of the poor. Don Quixote on the way to the windmills was hardly more exhilarated. Nevertheless, Vamper's peculiar oratory would certainly have driven him from the enterprise if in a normal condition. It was plentifully interlarded with jeering asides, intended for Chauncey's ear only.

"Onward, brave men, to the assured victory of the future! (And carry me on your splay-backs, will you?) We are engaged in the most glorious movement of modern times 'for the emancipation of the human race. (By the Great Moloch, I'd like to buy the gang for shipment to Cuba.) Let us urge on the revolution with ever increasing zeal. (Yes, revolve, revolve to the devil. Let's get an office.)"

"You're in a fair way to do that," suggested Chauncey, ironically.

"Fairish! 'Fair is foul and foul is fair,'" retorted Ishmael, in a sing-song. Suddenly breaking off, he looked keenly at his companion, and said with an inexpressibly confidential writhe of the lip—"Let's Shermanize."

"What?" asked Chauncey, bewildered.

"Sherman deals out Treasury money," explained the other, with dry suggestiveness.

"Our money! our money! robbed from us!" shouted the super-honest John, close behind, and others took up the cry.

Robert Chauncey opened his lips to protest, when a thought stopped his breath. Were not these poor creatures right after all? Why should they not regain by force of arms whatever had been taken from them by force of intellect, organization, and money? Could any one pretend that distribution had been fair and honest, when these men went in rags and others were revelling in all luxury? He raised himself to more than his usual height: the hour had come.

"We must have arms first—there they are," he cried, pointing to the Arsenal, which was now dimly visible.

Vamper looked at him in surprise, amusement, and pleasure. He had detested this young man unspeakably all along, and he did so even now that he was beginning to find in him a well-spring of sarcastic delight; but all the same it was a godsend to have an ally who was so ready to take hard knocks. For his own part, he had no idea of being at all inconsistent.

He exclaimed just loudly enough for Chauncey to hear—

"By all means! Let us storm! let us mount the battlements! let us burglarize!"

Then, raising his voice, he exhorted his partizans to hasten to a memorable and glorious victory.

But the catastrophe came more ignobly. In crossing the commons the mob had swollen and grown noisy, while heterogeneous weapons were freely brandished. A knot of policemen who had been following for some time, now hastened up, and charged them with scant ceremony.

But the odds were altogether too great. Though some of the negroes scattered, a considerable group stood firmly around their leaders; and the others soon rallied with so much outcry and turbulence that the policemen were beaten back faster and faster till their retreat ended in a dead run. Chauncey had kept on almost involuntarily with the pursuers; but when the Tiber (now made useful as a large sewer) was nearly reached, his sense of shame and absurdity revolted against this phase of revolution.

"Hang it!" he exclaimed, slackening his pace, "this is no good thing. I am not a beagle. Let's strike for the Arsenal."

"Go where glory waits thee," chanted Vamper.

"Dey done stop," said John, warily doing likewise, as he

saw Captain Hawksley, revolver in hand, critically observant on the crown of the arch ahead.

"Verily!" remarked Vamper, thoughtfully shifting his position so as to get behind his nearest adherent. 'O my prophetic soul, an ambuscade! a rally! At him, John!"

John needed little incentive, for he hated with a deadly hatred this hard, lordly man, who plainly regarded him as lower than any dog; beside he was wild with success. He gave a sort of inaudible growl, and rushed head foremost up the slope.

Hawksley, who was just about to aim at Vamper's astute head, turned a little with a look of vexation, and sent two bullets into his assailant. The first brought John to his knees; the second caught him as he staggered up, and sent him rolling to the foot of the mound; for the revolver was a large one and drove its weighty bullets with the force of a blow.

Captain Hawksley, as unconcerned outwardly as inwardly, cocked it again, and peered into the scattering crowd for Vamper. The latter was busy loading; but he discerned and fully appreciated that look.

"Now, Henry of Navarre, an oriflamme!" he cried.

But there was not the slightest need to urge Robert Chauncey forward. In the redoubtable statue-like figure before him he saw personified the egotistical, heartless cruelty which he fancied to be the dominant power of the land; and he recognized therein his successful rival also. He believed that this man of iron was backed by a strong force of ambuscaders. No matter, their rout would be the first victory of the new revolution; he would avenge at once the wrongs of himself, of the poor wretch writhing there, and of the downtrodden human race. One brilliant dash, and no one could doubt his heroic quality. The matter in hand was not at all to him the dislodging of a Virginia retrogressionist from a post which nobody really wanted. His sensations could have been no

9

more thrilling had he been about to dash with a brigade of
similarly infatuated spirits on the batteries of Balaclava.

With a slight sneer at Vamper's wise delay, he snatched
the pistol from the latter's hand, and sprang lightly up along
the edge of the arch.   His knowledge of such matters was
mainly theoretical, so the single shot that he fired while still in
motion went wide of any mark.   A moment later the unmov-
ing Hawksley had cooly shot him through the body not far
above the heart.

Robert Chauncey let his weapon fall, clasped his hand to
his side, staggering, and with the low, piteous words, "Oh,
my mother!" pitched headlong over the coping down to the
black waters below.   In that supreme moment, not a thought
of Jessica or philanthropy, the smiles of smooth-necked ladies
or the applause of uproarious men, the dainty shows or the
later fevers and phantasms of life!   His soul turned to that
long overlaid primal instinct, and the dear one now so far
away.

"After all, he *was* a gyallant gentleman," said Captain
Hawksley, slowly, with a strange mixture of relief and regret.
Then pity grew on him for the foolish young life which had
plunged with its one ruinous aspiration into that foul blackness; and when he looked abroad again for Vamper, to
whose account he laid this last dire evil also, there was a
hungry ferocity in his eye which might have interfered with
his aim.   But Ishmael had not trusted to this or to anything
except flight.   Indeed, the whole body of rioters, appalled by
such rapid and certain execution, had scattered beyond range.
A random shot or two came back from the moonlit distance.
While Hawksley walked away, disregarding them, he repeated more than once "A very gyallant young man."

CHAPTER XVIII.

When his enemy had certainly departed, Ishmael Vamper returned to see how his follower, John, was enjoying a bed of earth. He had not meant to extend his beneficence beyond this; but when the wounded man moaned out a request to be carried to a certain house, naming street and number, curiosity and possibly something more prompted him to supervise the transfer. Whether John had actually traced his mother back to Jessica's home or merely uttered the words which memory supplied to delirium, he had indicated the place of all others where Vamper would be most unwelcome.

Beside, Ishmael Vamper liked this Caliban of a convict, if it could be possible for him to like anybody. He had never yet found anything that was able to shock this partizan; and John's brutal cunning made him an appreciative and sometimes suggestive confidant. Best of all, John made no pretensions to any sort of decency or principle.

Accordingly Vamper called a few of his men together, and improvised a sort of stretcher whereon the wounded wretch was laid. As they were about starting, some one who had not seen the second shooting asked about "de udder white gen'lum."

"Gone a-fishing," answered Vamper, pointing significantly downward with a fantastic grimace; but the laughter was less general than he had expected.

Jessica, after her long reverie by the window, was crossing the hall on her way to the stairs when there came a violent knocking at the street door, and a call of, "Open fo' de Lord's sake!" She sprang impulsively to the door and opened it, but started back in alarm to make way for the wearied negroes, who staggered in with a great scuffling of feet, bearing their wounded comrade. The rush brought Vamper face to face with her, and at once he strove to take her hand; but appalled as she was at this ominous arrival, and breathless with the struggle between dismay and dignity, she yet was able to draw back out of reach, demanding—

"Must I call for the police?"

Vamper had begun to sneer, when like an echo he heard outside the same word, and the clatter of hoofs down the street. He knew that a squad of mounted policemen were in the act of dispersing his party. His only chance of escape was by the back way. With a single fruitless effort to snatch a kiss, he sprang away and hurried down the hall, pausing at the garden door to call, in mimicry of reassurance—

"Bewail not, Jessica. Of a surety, beloved, I return."

Jessica, as ever, seemed to find something not human in his varying fantastical uniqueness in taunting and troubling, and the grotesquely distorted quaintness of his words. But as she leaned against the wall shuddering and holding her heart, she found great comfort in the belief that his power to terrify and harm was vastly different from what it had been in that past of horrible memory. Probably she allowed too little for changed moods and surroundings; but her confidence was a guard in itself, and far more important than the accurate discrimination of its causes. It mattered little that her fancy played superstitiously with the coming and going of that ancestral ring. It mattered less that her undue susceptibility made her seem to hear low spirit murmurings of "Free! Free!"

Her trance was broken by a shriek from Mammy Charlotte who had just entered the hall.

"Oh, oh, oh!" she cried, falling on her knees in utter self-abandonment beside her son. "John, John, who done it?

Tell me, boy. Yo' hear? Tell me quick! Who done it?—hon', who done it?"

John roused a little at this frantic adjuration; and Jessica was coming forward to insist that he should not be injured by further outcry, when the weak answer, "Cap'n Hawksley," made her stop.

Charlotte rose with the tragic dignity of agony upon her, and began—

"Then may de good Lord curse——"

"Hush, Charlotte! Oh hush, Mammy!" cried Jessica, springing forward to stifle the imprecation.

"Oh, honey!" exclaimed Charlotte, pitifully, breaking down; and the two women wept side by side.

But they soon rallied to do what might be done for the stricken man. A surgeon was at once sent for and came promptly; but reported that John must die in a few hours, probably before morning. Charlotte, awed and terrified almost past sobbing, re-entered the room where he lay, and, seating herself by the bed, solemnly admonished him that the end was drawing near.

"I *knowd* it!" John responded, sulkily. Then, as if announcing the bitter result of a train of previous thought—for even he could think as he faced the on-coming of the great final shadow—he added, "I hain't got no use fo' none o' ye."

"Oh, John! John! It's *me*, John. You don't mean *me*, John?" cried his mother, interlocking her fingers and swaying from side to side.

His first reply was an inarticulate growl; but presently he uttered more distinctly, as if soliloquizing, "All agin me, dead agin me! Never hain't had no show!" Then, turning to his mother, he demanded savagely, "Why didn' yo' raise me better?"

"I wasn't there, John," answered Charlotte, weeping.

"Why not?" he pursued, sharply, though he must have known.

Charlotte's voice was choked, but she looked involuntarily

and piteously at her young mistress. Jessica bowed her head.
When she raised it, she was startled by the fell malevolence
of the gaze which the dying man had fixed on her.

"Curse 'em all!" he broke forth with sudden energy. "I
mout 'a' ben a man an' not a beast."

At this juncture a negro minister entered (having been duly
summoned by Charlotte), and John's thoughts turned to a
different channel. The alarm which his stolidity had at first
withstood was now rapidly deepening into panic, and he grew
frightfully anxious to "experience religion," or anything else
which would save him from that horror of great darkness and
torment which was his most salient conception of life beyond
death. So he readily joined in the crude religious services
which followed.

Jessica, finding that she was still a distracting and ire-pro-
voking influence, withdrew sadly to an adjoining room, where
she waited in silence any call for aid, with her mind inevitably
concentrated on that dire tragedy which had begun with the
beginning of her own life. Dwelling motionless on this idea
with strained inward gaze, she seemed to be aware of the
presence of a draped and misty greatness which had once
stepped from the background to close her plastic baby fingers
on the life of that other little soul, and thrust it down to a
wretched doom. The fancy was so full of indefinable menace
that she roused and shook herself bodily to throw it off; then
after one furtive, sidelong glance, summoned her attention to
the merely human sounds which came from about the death-
bed.

These seemed strange and bizarre enough even to one
familiar to such minstrelsy, though they did not startle or
shock her as they might have done at a first hearing. There
must always be something unearthly about religion; but in
this case the unearthliness was uncouth and barbaric as well.
The singers, in their zeal for snatching a deeply charred
brand from the burning, had soon discarded the ordinary
emotional hymns which they shared with the whites, and

passed to those abnormal productions of their own race in which the crude imaginings of a swart elder land and faith make themselves felt under Christian guise. In some passages there was a gruesome approach to the comical; in others, a familiar handling of sacred things that was saved from blasphemy only by their obvious sincerity; while in others, the incongruity of the refrain distorted or even inverted the meaning.

Yet, on the whole, in spite of dislocations and monstrosities, these songs of the soul were uniquely impressive a· she heard them, for they dealt intensely with the great unchanging tragic lights and shadows—sin and evil, life and punishment, and hope outlasting all. There was a quality in them which suggested a child at play among the secrets o.· the universe; but terror was never absent.

The first words that reached her were:

> "I year a rumblin' under de groun';
> It mus' be Satan, a turnin' aroun'.
> I year a rumblin' up in de sky;
> It mus' be Jesus a passin' by."

The next hymn was sung zealously, with a mingling of triumph and pathos in the refrain. It began:

> "Saint Michael an' de dragon—
> Don't ye grieve after me;
> I don't want ye to grieve after me."

So one followed another, the excitement of all the singers rapidly increasing, until they seemed going by clockwork— the preacher bowing and stamping, the mother dizzily swaying, and even the form on the bed jerking spasmodically in time to the vehemently expelled words. A sense of frantic physical contest was conveyed by the whole scene; they were working furiously up to a predetermined climax. At last it was reached, and with a zealous accompaniment of "Praise de Lor'" and "Amen! Glory! Amen!" from his stimulating com-

panions, the dying man began to shout and scream ecstatic-
ally.

"I hab Jesus!" he shrieked, laboring for breath, "I hab
Him! I hab Him!" at the same time grappling in the air as if
to seize some tangible presence. Then, with a shrill outcry
of "Glory! Glory! Hallelujah! Glory!" he flung himself
upward and forward—and dropped back dead.

And immediately a cock crew from a neighboring enclos-
ure—as his kind often will in the dark, silent hours, for no
observable cause—with a wild, rollicking, irrational jubilation.

"He must 'a' seen a great light," murmured Mammy Charlotte, in a hush of awe and hope.

"Amen, Amen!" responded the preacher, in somber joy.

Jessica wondered at them. That inflated caricaturing fal-
setto, so derisively echo-like, struck painfully across her
morbidly exalted perceptions, and made her gasp. She had
an undefined and needless dread of something worse to follow. So, urged by the instinct of escape, she rose unsteadily
and worked her way to her own room, with the face of Vamper staring at her from every window-pane that she passed,
like a revelation from the abyss.

She paused only to light the gas-jets and turn them to their
fullest glare; then lay down without undressing, finding relief in the silence and brightness, but too deeply distressed
and shaken to think connectedly or to have any clearly outlined feeling. After the lapse of an hour or so, she heard the
approach of Mammy Charlotte's rheumatic halting footsteps.
Dreading the interview, Jessica closed her eyes and lay perfectly quiet. The steps entered the room, drew near ever so
gently, and ceased. Charlotte had taken her seat patiently by
the bedside. At intervals a hushed sigh came from her. Before long Jessica found herself weeping.

"I thought you were asleep, honey," said the old nurse.

Jessica rose on her elbow, "What is it you want to say to
me, Mammy?"

Charlotte sat in silence a few moments longer with the grey dawn making her face seem ghastly.

" I knows it'll be hard," she said at last. Then after another pause, " I hain't nobody but *you* now, honey." Then a pause again, and the question, " Is you 'gwine to get rid o' me, Miss Jessie?"

" Why, Mammy, what do you mean?" Jessica exclaimed in a little flutter of dread, half foreseeing what was to come.

" You knows what he done tole me when dey brought him in," said Charlotte quietly. Then, with more bitterness and tremor in her voice, she continued," " You knows who done it, Miss Jessie. Will you marry dat man?"

Jessica had been arguing it over inarticulately. She now gave her arguments form, and made them audible.

"Charlotte, I grieve for you and with you; but we must be just. If Captain Hawksley shot John, it surely must have been in self-defence. You know—painful as it is to say so—what have been his modes of life, his associates, his own acts of violence. If he attacked the captain, what was the captain to do?"

But Charlotte was a bereaved mother, and reasoned from the heart only. She asked with a sort of intense gentleness—

" Don't you see, honey, dat I can't come to live wid de man dat killed my son? Why his hands would look red every time I sot eyes on 'em."

Jessica shuddered, uttering a little groan; and Mammy Charlotte began again with increasing emotion:

"An' if John *was* bad, who took him away fum me, an' give all his life to de devil? All but his las' hour, tank de Lor'! An' dey give *you* to me instead, honey; an', oh, I ha' growed to lub you so dese many many years! An' now dey've done kill him, an' 'll take you away too! Oh, Miss Jessie, you'll *never* do it. *Don't* do it. De Lord won't bless it, 'deed He won't. All de many years dat I've lived wid you, honey! Have pity for your mother's sake on your poor ole mammy."

The controversy between feeling and logic did not proceed much farther. Jessica had foreknown the issue; for after all she had loved Mammy Charlotte first and longest, and the claim for atonement strengthened the claim on sympathy. Beside, with all her theoretical justifying of the captain, there was something very shocking and hard to explain away in that suffering, dying fellow-man (twice shot through) as he had lain so lately before her eyes. This by itself would not have withstood that other concrete fact, Captain Hawksley with his manly presence and earnest plea. It was Charlotte's vehement entreaty that finally turned the scale against him.

CHAPTER XIX.

"CAN I CLASP IT REEKING RED?"

Captain Hawksley had determined to give himself up to the police the next morning to answer any charges which might be preferred; but he thought it best to call first upon Jessica and explain. He was surprised to find an unusual gloom about the house; and when Jessica entered the parlor the mournful distance of her manner filled him with vague alarm.

"That was a sad affair, Captain Hawksley—that of last night," she said, hopelessly.

Hawksley, thinking of Robert Chauncey, answered, "Ah, you have heard of it! I would have spared him, if I could, as your friend."

"My friend," she exclaimed, her distress yielding to astonishment.

"I certainly supposed so," he replied, with a surprised air. "At all events, he was a gyallant gentleman."

Here every graver sentiment yielded to a sense of incongruity. A puzzled smile flitted into her face and out again, and she asked:

"What in the world do you mean?"

"I mean, Miss Armstrong, that Mr. Robert Chauncey——" he began rather austerely.

"He, too!" she cried, almost in a shriek.

Hawksley looked at her bewildered. He had temporarily forgotten the negro. Before his mind had fully adjusted itself to her point of view, she spoke again in a constrained voice.

"Well, sir, tell me all about it, if you please. Are there any more victims?"

In reply he explained proudly and frankly, with no appearance of contrition, exactly what had happened.

"Surely you must see, Miss Armstrong," he added, with offended precision of utterance, "that I was perfectly justified in all I did."

She made no response, though he kept looking interrogatively into her down-dropped eyelids.

At last he exclaimed, with displeased impatience, "I am sure you do not wish for a husband who would not defend himself or *you*."

But Jessica did not even look up. She was thinking of Robert Chauncey's bereaved mother, and how the news would reach her before very long. She was thinking, too, of Mammy Charlotte; and of her own blighted hopes. It was not possible for her to answer at once.

Her lover, watching her closely, began to grow fiercely jealous.

"Perhaps you would rather *I* should have died," he suggested with stately bitterness.

"Oh no, no!" she replied. "How can you say that, Archer?"

It was the first time she had ever addressed him by his christian name. His face brightened with joy and hope, and, forgetting her recent coldness and censure, he caught her in his arms and kissed her lips passionately. She could not repel him, with the vision which his words had called up still plainly before her; but even while receiving his caresses she could not shut out that other vision of the old nurse's frantic despair and her own solemn promise. She felt as though she were weakly suffering a curse to settle upon all of them. As soon as she could, she requested with grave dignity—

"Release me, sir, if you please."

He did so, and she withdrew to a more distant seat. His face grew dark.

"Am I or am I not your affianced husband, Miss Armstrong?"

"You are not, Captain Hawksley," she replied, in a low tone, making a brave effort to look steadily at him.

"What?" he exclaimed, hardly believing his ears.

"That is," she added, by way of qualification, "unless you insist when the lady wishes release."

"Such has not been my kiaracter," he replied, loftily. "But you will admit that I am at least entitled to an explanation." Then, breaking down, "What is it? Do you blame me, Jessica? Oh, my darling, do you not love me? See, I have even brought the ring—I was so sure——"

The gathering trouble in his voice had reached a tremor of agony. It shook her, sympathetically, too. She began to yield.

"Captain Hawksley," she said, rising in some alarm; then hesitated to steady her voice, and at last went on, "I will *not* blame you. I *do* care for you. I am too much shaken by recent events to say more now. But I will write. And—it is all over—good-bye—forgive—forget."

He rose as if to rush toward her; but she checked him with decision, saying—

"It is all over, sir."

His face paled, then flushed again.

"Tell me," he demanded, imperiously, "do I owe this to that—I mean to the late Mr. Chauncey."

"No, sir," she answered, in displeased surprise, turning toward the door.

"Wait one moment," he cried, all that was worst in his arrogant temper coming uppermost; "Are you throwing me over on account of that black brute and his lachrymose surviving relatives? Am I discyarded to please a nigger?"

Her pride and scorn were not less than his as she replied—

"Yes, sir."

He looked thunder and lightning for a moment, then said
slowly—

"I can dispense with the letter, then. A gyurl like you is
no wife for a Virginia gentleman, Miss Armstrong."

She held her peace, inwardly pitying the distress which
could cause such rudeness.

As he reached the door he hesitated, then turned with a
decorous, controlled face and came two steps back, bowing
rigidly.

"Miss Armstrong," he said, "I owe an apology to both of
us. I have spoken as no gentleman should speak to a lady.
I had not adequately realized the effect of the progressive
ideas of the day. For your own sake I hope you will at last
diskyard them. I beg your pardon, Miss Armstrong."

She bowed, and he departed, striding fiercely up the street.
But at the second corner he halted, at war with himself, wondering whether he had done all that he ought to have done as
a gentleman and a man of honor; wondering, too, if he could
yet do anything to win back that woman who was so inesti-
mably dear to him. Dear! he would give his immortal soul
if he could but have her. "Inordinate affection!" perhaps he
had always been inordinate; inordinate, for that matter, in the
defense of Church and creed and the old religious landmarks;
and he would not ask pardon even of God for consistency. Pardon! it was beyond volition, a great upheaving need in the foundations of his nature. It shook, and strained, and tortured him
with vain craving. Yet how equably she could displace him!
with what propriety of sympathetic concern! with what nicely
adjusted reluctance, barely a trifle too light to counterbalance
a bit of clap-trap sentiment! What was there of heart-warm
human affection in that? What of the adorable clinging passion of womanly love which sends its rootlets deep into two
souls, and will not suffer them to be torn apart in life or
in death! He began to writhe against her, and despise her,
and doubly despair of her, even while his irrational longing
grew deeper and stronger. He had never been a man who

made allowances for others, and he made none now. The
absorbing and unchanging devotion of his own nature demanded an equal return; he might as well have demanded an
earthquake or an epic.

Yet at that moment Jessica was sobbing and weeping in
most dismal sincerity both for his sake and her own. She
was doubting in fitful, shaken gusts of feeling not only the propriety and kindness but the uprightness of the course she had
taken; half wishing that he would return and give her one
more chance; wholly certain that she could never love another or be happy again.

Hawksley's mind turned naturally in its wrath of bereave-
ment and outrage to the main-spring of his troubles, the
execrated spirit of innovation—and Vamper. He had some
plausible grounds for regarding it as that technical " wrath of
the righteous " which is supposed to take extreme measures
out of the jurisdiction of conscience. In Vamper he recognized, more confidently than ever, the leering whisperer
behind the scenes who wrought all the evil which had lately
been woven across and about his path. Perhaps it was only
a new manifestation of a primitive human instinct when
brought face to face with the startling problems of sin—an
instinct that embalmed its teaching long ago in those still
surviving forms of indictment which deal with theories of in-
stigation. A spirit, whether embodied or bodiless, which
aspires to the *rôle* of prompter must expect to be a scapegoat.
Hawksley decided to postpone settlement with the law until
another item should have been added to the account.

At any other time this might not have been a matter of
choice; but disorder was in the air then, and its effects were
felt everywhere. As he approached the centres of business,
one newsboy after another ran down the street, zigzagging to
reach eager customers, and shouting vehemently. Their frag-
mentary, half-articulate outcries came to him like a summons
from a world of blood and fire, such as he had known before,
which would not suffer him to remain away. Moreover, it

was pretty certain to draw into its vortex the enemy whom he
specially sought.   Thus a combination of motives directed
him to the nearest railway depot.   He reached it just in time
to see a train of cars, bound northward, whisk away as if by
magic; while the unmistakable figure of Ishmael Vamper
stepped out on the rear platform and bowed with a ceremo-
nious reproduction of Captain Hawksley's own manner.   Then
he kissed his hand and waved it airily, calling out in a mirthful, reassuring sing-song, a homely phrase of adieu which he
had probably picked up on the Eastern Shore—"So, Captain."

Hawksley can hardly have intended to reply into a crowded
car; but instinct or habit sent his hand to his hip.   Others
noted the movement, and a finger was laid—very gingerly—
on his shoulder, while a voice said in tremulous deprecation,
"Boass!"

Hawksley's ear caught the African intonation, and he strode
violently aside as if to fling off something venomous.   His
face did not grow more amiable as he discovered that he had
been accosted by a negro in uniform.

The latter, disconcerted, did his best to conciliate, saying—

"I wasn' studyin' toe 'sturb you boss.   I didn' go for to be
persumptious.   But I was 'feard I mought be bleedg toe take
yo inter custad-ee, boss."

"I think not," answered Hawksley, with grim significance.

"No, boss," protested the policeman, hastily, at once changing front, "mos' reliably not!   No such attention, I do 'sho'
you, boss!   I haben't fo'got dat I owe yo' my salvation, boss—
my nocturnal salvation."

"Were you one of the crowd who were making such uncommonly good time?" asked Hawksley with relaxing face·

"'Deed I was, boss," answered the policeman, chuckling.
"I was fo' a fac'.   Dat peril will dwell in my membranes, sar,
forever and ever, amen.   I haven' done been so scared, boss,
since I was converted an' got de grace an' de power.   I felt
like a backslidin' sinner wid de devil arter him "

"A very good presentation of the situation, all round," endorsed Hawksley.

" Yess, boss, heaps of 'em," assented the other, with cheery vagueness, glad to do the polite in his turn.

The crowd, which had begun to gather in the hope of seeing something dramatic, now dispersed with a disappointed air. Nevertheless, the well-meaning fellow lowered his voice confidentially, as he continued—

" Pow'ful pity 'bout dat nice tipsy young gen'l'um, boss! Evil communications, boss! Pourin' ole wine into young bottles, boass!" And this sage in uniform gave his head the true moralizing shake. He was considered a very improving exhorter at the "colored people's Ebenezer," and never felt greater t an when expatiating in full regalia to The Amalgamated Sons and Daughters and Brothers and Sisters of Moses.

Hawksley did not smile this time. The expounder resumed—

" It was a dee-up jedgment—ah; it went right froo him. He succumbed in de darkness, ah. Praise de Lord, ah, who done raise him fum de valley o' de shadows, wid a sorter bung hole in he side an' moughty nasty an' stinkin'!"

" What!" exclaimed Hawksley, " is he still alive?"

" He *am.*"

The orator was going on, but Hawksley stopped him, ejaculating, " Thank God!" with solemn emphasis, raising his hat slowly at the same time, as if in some august presence. Then he asked—

" Where is he?"

" In a little shanty, boss," was the answer. " His punctuation was so bad de doctor wouldn't let us export him to de horse-spittle. He jess stood out an' wouldn't."

" Who extracted him from that horrible place?"

" I dunno who 'stracted him, boss, but I done help fotch him out. He was a hangin' on a rope, sar, when we come back in fo'ce, after you—removed yourself, sar; a danglin'

10

mos' like a big mud catfish on a string—an' a openin' his mouf *so*." Here he made a very idolatrous and Polynesian exhibi- tion.

Captain Hawksley turned aside and said curtly, "Go on."

"Well, boss," continued the narrator more hastily, "he 'lowed he wouldn' let go. He hung on like a dentis' toe a bad toofe. But we yanked him out bes' way we could, an' we done tote him toe de fuss house, a cavortin' wid de misery an' a talkin' mos' unwisely. Den de sisters done come an' makes him salubrious, an' now he's a lyin' as peaceable as Lazarus in Abraham's bosom—leastways 'ceptin' de nice hair mattress mus' be comfortabler dan de ole man's shirt studs."

"So the Catholics have him," said the captain, in a not very gracious tone, which may have been more or less ancestral; "well, will you be kyind enough to show me the way?" handing over a little silver.

"I dunno, boss," answered the policeman, looking furtively around. "It's ofe my beat." Then he pocketed the coin. "Never mind, boss, I'll do it. It does me good toe meet up wid a ole time, high tone Vaginny gen'l'um, an' year him say 'keind' wid dat lofty intoenashin. It revives 'membranes of de quality, sar. Dats de way our white folks allers talked. An', besides, boss, I have not forgotten an' I shall not forget my nocturnal salivation, sar."

CHAPTER XX.

A toilsome walk across the commons brought Captain Hawksley to the wind-rattled frame building wherein Robert Chauncey was to make the most of his slippery hold on life—so like that of the dangling squirrel which sees (or feels) the sunshine through his dripping blood and keeps yet a little longer, hardly by will or choice, the one last grip which stays his frolicsome being from the fall into utter darkness!

Hawksley was pleased to find that the rather squalid inhabitants had been induced to give up their best room, and the good "sister" who now sat by the bedside had made that best very much better. Divers little articles of comfort were there, looking like exotics, and everything was clean, even to the bed and its coverlet. By one of those untimely and altogether improper excursions of thought which spare no one, the captain reflected that it would be a great comfort to Robert Chauncey to die neatly and tastefully, if he must die at all. Yet as he looked at the thin, pale face, hardly in relief against the pillow, it did not seem to him that this young man could be merely dilettante or over-fastidious. Perhaps he saw rather the pain and the weakness than their possessor—eternal things which have impressiveness enough to lend it.

The sister saw that he was pausing as if in some perplexity; so she rose and came forward, with a glance at the patient and a quiet warning gesture. They passed out

through the door and far enough for the sigh and drone
of the rising wind to drown their voices. Her Celtic face
had in a measure prepared Hawksley for her first utterance;
yet if he had been accessible to any romantic illusions they
would have been promptly dispelled.

" Sure," said she, " ye'll be wan av the poor by's frinds,
that we've been a tryin' to find, and couldn't, more's the
pity ?"

After a moment's hesitation, he answered—

" Yes." Then frankly, " It is right you should know; I
shot him."

"Oh, Mither o' mercy !" she cried, drawing back. "An' is
that what ye call bein' frindly!"

" We will not dwell on that," he said, with distant gentleness. " You are not my confessor, you know."

"Aha, but it'll be a hard penance he'll give ye, sor !" she
cried, with exultant relish ; then as if it were qualified by
doubt, she asked—

" But maybe ye're not a Catholic ?"

" I am not," he replied, " but I bear my penance may be—
rightly or wrongly. However, I assure you I come as a friend.
You may stand gyard over us both."

She hovered doubtfully about him as they re-entered.
Chauncey was still asleep. The captain deliberately took a
tablet from his pocket and pencilled a short note ; then tore
off the page methodically, folded it, wrote the direction on
the back and handed it to his fellow-watcher.

" Send this as soon as you can," he said. " It will bring a
friend who will never forsake *him*." He could not refrain
from laying a little bitter emphasis on the last word.

The sister looked at it and at him, then raised it to the
light, and read aloud with some difficulty, " Miss Jes—sica
Armstrong. Turning, she asked—

" Is it *her* ye'll be maning ?"

The name seemed to have reached the sleeper, for he stirred
a little and his lips seemed to be forming it, though no sound

issued. Hawksley saw this and was undeniably stung, though his resolution did not falter. The curiosity in the sister's manner also nettled him, though in a different spot. So he replied with unusual curtness—

"You're waking him. Make haste, that's a good gyurl."

She bristled with umbrage at the word "girl," however transformed, and at the tone in which it was uttered. They recalled old kitchen and laundry days before the era of white caps and black raiment. Her self-assertion was quite wasted, for he did not even look at her, perceiving which her wrath doubled, and she came very near making an irreligious flounce of bottled fury on her way to the door.

Her incautious movements completed Chauncey's awakening. His eyes unclosed, and he murmured something about Cypress Beach. Then recognition came more unmistakably into them, and he said in a low welcoming voice, "Captain Hawksley."

"He sames plazed!" exclaimed the sister, who had now returned to the bedside, and whose anger was already giving place to her interest in the affairs of her charge.

"He doesn't remember," said Hawksley. "Yes, Mr. Chauncey, it is I." Then he murmured half aloud, "What ought I to do?"

"Hold your pays! It's a blessed thing he forgot that same," cried the sister, almost fiercely.

Their words set Chauncey's mind feebly in motion, like one groping with outspread fingers in a darkened passage. Back it went into a chaos of thick darkness and effluvia, and no sensations but of struggling and whirling and choking; then on to a desperate, interminable clinging with hands and chin, while his head swam and a great pain tore at his side; then back to a sudden fall from some great height; and then on again to slowly ebbing hours and kind, strange forms and faces. One by one these visions seemed to come of themselves and shift about waveringly. He could not be quite sure which was first or which was last, or what was their thread of connection—if any of them had ever really been. He did not particularly care about the explanation, or indeed about anything.

Then more vividly he saw that tableau on the archway; Vamper and his wretched crew behind, John writhing under foot, Hawksley rigid in front, and himself as a sort of centre-piece rushly blindly forward and upward in what now seemed a faintly amusing turmoil of passion; while below him the unspeakably nasty sewer-creek waited innocently for any one who was fool enough to tumble into it.

He inspected that picture as dispassionately as a connoissieur or a scientific investigator, although there was nothing of conscious will in the scrutiny. It was all a show to him now. He knew perfectly what had brought him into that panorama, but he knew it as the experience of an unaccountably foolish young man, whom he almost thought of in the third person. The interests which had been so real and thrilling then were strangely faded now. He did not feel as though he owned any serious grievance. There was something so preposterous about the masquerade that the catastrophe seemed quite in order. He smiled placidly to think how the whole episode would work up into a caricature.

That smile was still on his face when he looked towards Hawksley and said—

" No, I have not forgotten."

" You forgive me? you are glad to see me?" asked Hawksley with a touch of eagerness.

" Yes, so far as a fellow can be glad of anything. I have been a *blessed* ass; and yet just now I believe I could forgive even myself."

" You are a noble man," exclaimed Hawksley; " I said at the time you were a gyallant gentleman."

" Did you? How uncommonly kind! If I could only have heard you!"—and Chauncey's face made a pathetic attempt to be mildly comical. Nevertheless the captain's praise gratified him.

The sly irony did not altogether escape Hawksley's notice (though he was never quick to suspect ridicule), and at another time he might have been offended; but now it rather gave him pleasure, as putting them on terms of acknowledged comradeship and good will. He did not like to feel that there was any unkindness between himself and the man whom he had shot. Most assuredly there was none on his part.

These sentiments were not lost on Robert Chauncey, as he lay there with nothing but hazy perceptions to occupy either mind or body. The humorous element of the situation entered and floated about in his brain like mist in moonlight, making everything else seem as unsubstantial as itself, and prolonging his gentle smile till it seemed as though this had come to stay. Presently, however, it faded, and he spoke as one who is impelled by duty, yet bears willing testimony.

"Sister," said he, "you have been very kind to me; and I know you will do me one more kindness. If I die—and I daresay I had better, for the world can get on tolerably without me—I want you to remember that _he_ did this in self-defence."

He pointed weakly to his side and glanced at Hawksley as he spoke.

"You're jist an angel," she rather irrelevantly replied, beginning to dig at her eyes with her handkerchief.

This time there came from the bed a sound like a far away echo of laughter. Hawksley had taken Chauncey's hand and was pressing it with grateful respect, when he felt it twitch, and the laughter ceased. He looked at the sufferer's face, and it _was_ a sufferer's face indeed.

"This is frightful," said he.

"It is no good thing," admitted Chauncey, gasping a little.

"You must be more kyareful," cautioned the all but fatal friend; "we have been talking too volubly."

"One might as well die smiling as sulking," replied Chauncey, with an effort.

Then he was dutifully silent for awhile. When he again

spoke, it was evident that with the revival of his vital spirits some other things had revived which were not so pleasant. We regain life as we keep it, under penalties.

"There's one thing, Captain," he said, with rather forced magnanimity. "Speaking of angels—I suppose a fellow who is about leaving may say it—don't be too hard on *her* if she isn't quite *that*. Few women are, you know. She may need some practice to get your precision of aim, even in religious matters; and her enthusiasms of all sorts are perhaps a little more comfortable and loosely worn than yours. They may not happen to gall her when they gall you, and then the family won't be quite unanimous. You see I can face the inevitable all round.

"And after all," he added, wearily, "it doesn't matter much. Nothing in this world matters very much. I'm pretty well out of the game."

Captain Hawksley was breathless for a moment. He forgot everything else in the unconscious irony of the other's words. He to be advised and yielded to as the victor, when his disastrous failure had destroyed the whole value of life!

He said stiffly, almost sternly, "You are quite in error, sir. I shall never see that lady again, though she has my sincere regyard. It is *you* who will have to show consideration." After hesitating a moment he added more cordially, "I wish all happiness and prosperity to you both. Do not feel hurt if she sometimes remembers me kyindly while you are in the sunshine, and I—am out of it."

Here the good sister began to shake like so much faintly ruddy blancmange; and she observed demurely—

"It sames to me that yees two gintlemen are moighty kind an' thoughtful to one anither, a givin' the young lady back an' forth like a battledore an' shettlecock. But av nayther of ye will have her, out of pure good will, how can the ither one get her? And thin—may be she won't have aither of ye at all at all."

Robert Chauncey smiled, but said nothing.

Captain Hawksley declared, "There is good sense in what our discriminating friend says. As for dying, diskyard such fancies. There is no reason why you should die. *You* have not seen the end of all you believed in and held dear."

The next moment he looked ashamed of this instinctive appeal for sympathy, and then resumed his usual composure of countenance.

The sister evidently did not approve of his choice of topics.

"Ye may come an' see him to-morrow, sir," she said, significantly.

He bade Chauncey "Good-bye" encouragingly, pressing his hand as he rose.

The patient faintly returned the pressure, with tears in his eyes, and said—

"God bless you! I never half understood you before."

The sister followed Hawksley outside. He turned considerately toward her.

"Indade, I'm thinkin' the praist might let up on the penance thin," she said.

He shook his head sedately. "There is not much 'letting up' in the universe short of the Day of Judgment—if *then*. Well, my good woman, take this for his benefit. Say nothing, but get what he requires. If there is more than you can use for him keep it for your poor."

Hawksley strode rapidly away while she was overhauling in some bewilderment the liberal roll of paper money which he had handed her. She looked from it to him, and from him to it again.

"I wandre now," she said, bowing her head over it in loose jerks as if she were a great wire-neck doll, "I wandre whether that same is an angel, too. He gives away his money like a seraphim."

CHAPTER XXI.

"WHEN PAIN AND ANGUISH WRING THE BROW."

For an hour or more after Hawksley's departure, Jessica had been self-imprisoned in her room, refusing to answer a word to Mammy Charlotte's anxious summons and entreaties. It was possible to forego her lover, but not to forego some futile, pettishly vindictive token of conscious ill-usage. She wished almost savagely that the gravity of her sacrifice might be felt.

Indeed, she *was* desolate. She felt that she had irrevocably cast away her only reliance; she dared not stay unprotected in these ominous times, in danger of Vamper's molestation; and how could she present herself again at Cypress Beach? One distress had followed another, until everything in the world seemed working together for evil.

While she was in this dismal reverie, she heard her uncle's voice under her window, and immediately afterward a clearly emphasized stroke of their heavy knocker. Acting on her first impulse, she sprang to the door, unlocked it, and hurried downstairs to welcome him; but in the hall below she was visited by disabling memories, and shrank back in doubt if not in fear. At last, as he was admitted, she summoned all her strength, and went straight up to him. He held out both his hands, advancing with a face full of sunbeams, and the cheery greeting—

"Well, Jessica, how do you come on?"

Jessica stared for a moment; she *had* been "coming on" with a vengeance. But the next moment all else was lost in

a great rush of relief and delight, and she began to laugh,
though a little nervously.

He joined in her mirth, patting her gently on the back, and
kissing her forehead. He had obviously determined to set
aside all disagreeable matters as if they had never been. So
he discoursed to her voluminously on the state of the country,
the precarious condition of Baltimore, the agricultural prospects of the season, the constantly increasing laziness of "labor," the promising attributes of his latest thoroughbred colt,
and the peculiar fattening qualities of his neighbor's pigs; but
not a word about Vamper or even Hawksley.

Before this heavy strategy could be fairly tested, it was
suddenly thrown into disorder by little Prince. That very
young gentleman was not much in the habit of interrupt-
ing, but now the stress of curiosity and interest could not
be withstood. After long fidgeting and sundry abortive endeavors (which were absolutely overwhelmed, without notice,
in the flood of the old gentleman's oracular eloquence), he at
last found a real break in the monologue, and interjected,
scramblingly—

"I say, Cousin Jess, is it true the captain shot some strikers
or somebody last night? A man told us so. I disremember
his name."

"Unhappily he did," answered Jessica.

"Unhappily!" repeated Prince, with some indignation.
"Do you suppose if a gang of men came at me with clubs
and pistols I would fire in the air? Ha, you catch me if I
would!"

But Jessica was rising, unsteadily, to escape torture.

"One of them was an old friend—Mr. Chauncey," she said.
"The death of the other has driven Captain Hawksley—from
—this house——"

At this point the tremor of her lips and throat became
uncontrollable, and she suddenly buried her face in her hands,
shaking with violent sobs.

Her uncle sprang heavily to his feet, with an angry side-

glance at Prince, and drew her into his arms, laying her cheek
against his great chest and bowing his well-bearded face and
great head obliquely over her, with much caressing and purring, like a Lybian lion comforting its wounded young.
Then he looked up again, demanding, sternly—

"Can you not be more considerate in your allusions, boy?"

"Considerate!" grumbled Prince, with an injured air.
"Haven't I upset three fellows for talking about Cousin
Jessie? Don't you call that 'considerate'?"

Luckily, Jessica's ears were too well muffled to catch this
reassuring speech. Presently Prince's conscience stung him,
and he crept up sheepishly alongside, saying—

"I didn't go to hurt your feelings, Cousin Jessie. 'Deed,
'n' double 'deed, I didn't."

Then Jessica withdrew a little and shook off her tears, so to
speak—

"This Jessica of yours is a foolish little goose, you see,"
she said, with a mournful archness; "but you know how I
love you both. Sit down, and I will try to tell you about it."

When she had made an end of her story, her uncle added
the moral.

"It all springs from this agrarian and communistic agitation, which is a reverberation of abolitionism—a most noxious
influence. But what could·have made that promising young
man league with rahscals, and throw away his life gratuitously
in so despicable a cause? It is inexplicable, radically inexplicable. As for John, he always seemed to me a devil—a
natural devil; but you say he died in faith and hope; and,
after all, what human heart is for ever exempt from the goad-
ings of compunction and the influx of laudable propensities?
At all events, Charlotte has been a faithful servitor, and we
owe it to her that every decorum should be observed in her
son's interment. If we can help her to organize a fine dis-
play, it will be a prodigious consolation."

With all his kindliness, he could not help smiling a little.

In their absorbing conversation, a timid rap at the outer

door, and its opening, had passed unnoticed. Hawksley's letter was now brought in to Jessica. She glanced over it trembling; then uttered a little joyful cry—

" He is not dead!"

" My hat! Zincs and death, my hat! Where *did* I put my hat?" exclaimed Mr. Armstrong, rising and looking eagerly in the most unlikely places. Then he paused to ask, "Where is the poor young fellow, my dear?"

Jessica was in a strange state of indecision. She did not really mean to neglect her suffering friend; but she had a fore-feeling of the epochal nature of this visit, with regard to her own future, which involved a certain shrinking, even rebellion. Even amid her startled delight at the news that one suitor was saved from death and the other from being his homicide, she detected (or suspected) in Hawksley's note a displeasing intimation of unauthorized, cavalier transfer. Surely it was very humiliating to find her affections handed about as current coin of generosity, and all the more so for certain inward whispers that she might have to ratify the transaction. Yet circumstances would not permit her to halt. Already the world, as represented by her uncle and cousin, was beginning to open its eyes over her delay. So she postponed all thoughts of resistance, and drifted with the current —to Robert Chauncey.

When that fortunately unfortunate young man came hazily out of slumber, to feel his sweetheart's light hand smoothing the hair from his brow, he began to grow perceptibly better. He had no doubt now that it was his purpose to get well. He looked up at her gratefully, and asked—

" Is there any feasable plan for getting the worst of a shooting match once or twice a week?"

She laid her finger on his lips with a motherliness which he found both diverting and delightful.

" I am not a sensitive plant or a bird of paradise, though you may think I look like it," he remarked, perversely, as well as that finger would let him. But he saw so much gen-

uine concern in her face that he closed his eyes with a faintly
comical grimace, and seemingly went to sleep.

As he lay thus shamming, half in lassitude and half in
artfulness, a steady stertorous breathing, varied by occasional
wakeful starts and breaks, came from beyond the foot of the
bed. Through his closed eyelids Chauncey seemed to see
Mr. Armstrong succumbing, after a period of irradiation, to
the prolonged quiet of the scene, and bowing his head mas-
sively on his breast like Jove dozing on Olympus. Somehow
Robert felt more in sympathy with the old gentleman than
ever before; but the portrait tickled his fancy so that it nearly
broke up the repose of his expression.

A moment later the sister, perhaps in search of less sleepy
surroundings, rose and passed out with the very faintest of
creaking and rustling. The occupants of the room were thus
reduced to the sleeper, the seeming sleeper, and the young
lady who was most obviously wide awake. Silence, except
for Mr. Armstrong's premonitions of snoring, and a faint, un-
decided fluttering in another quarter, seemed to deepen and
dwell about them, until Robert Chauncey's wits were really
drifting away in a haze that was rather tinged than broken by
a certain formless expectation.

In this state he felt, or thought he felt, what he was desiring
most of all things, the momentary pressure of two warm
velvety lips, recalling his senses from dreamland. With com-
mendable discretion he kept his eyes still sealed, but could
not quite control a certain lighting and flushing of countenance, a tell-tale tremor and thrill. While the print of the
caress (real or fancied) was still on his brow, he heard Jessica
move about the room; and felt, without seeing it, that he was
undergoing a furtive and uneasy inspection from various
points of view.

If Jessica were responsible for this little phenomenon, no
one ever knew it certainly. At any rate, neither Chauncey's
lady-love nor his creative imagination kissed him again during his illness.

In truth, Jessica was deeply stirred by pity, and somewhat more. Deep as had been her distress at the loss of Captain Hawksley, sincere as was her reluctance to allow one image to supplant another with such unseemly speed, these considerations had altogether vanished at the sight of that helpless, untimely smitten form, that wan, weak, patient face, so meanly housed yet so cheerily willing to endure and forgive. Logical justifications might be very satisfying to the intellect; but the man who received the bullet had an undeniable advantage over the one who sped it, when the appeal lay elsewhere; especially as the latter was absent and intact, in body and conscience. Moreover, she surmised something of her own influence in bringing about the disaster; and she felt that the importance thus accorded her was in sharp contrast with Hawksley's depreciating readiness to forego all further efforts. It was something to be a motive to somebody. Nevertheless she did not spare herself for the scornful lack of perception which had driven the man who held her dearest into the very jaws of death.

She could not go with her uncle in denouncing as utterly despicable the cause in which Robert Chauncey had suffered. She saw undoubtedly that grave dangers lurked in it, and that excesses would almost certainly ensue; but her mind was better prepared than ever before to admit a baleful picture of the oppressions which might have been long endured in silence by multitudes practically outside of her world and her knowledge. Captain Hawksley's stronghold had been in her enthusiastic adoration of heroism; but perhaps after all the heroism of the heart appealed to her more strongly than the heroism of tradition and conviction. She found something finer and worthier of homage in self-sacrifice on behalf of the wronged, however short-sighted and illogical, than in the iron-nerved championing of any human arrangements or order of things whatsoever.

When Robert Chauncey judged it safe to awake, she was examining some trifle with a neutral expression of countenance, and not even a flush that he could be sure of. At the same time Mr. Armstrong revived suddenly, and his broad, sunny face beamed paternally upon him.

"I hope you are refreshed by your repose, sir," said he.

"Very much," answered Robert. "This sort of thing will soon make me well."

There was an encouraging elasticity in his voice, perhaps there was an involuntary tone of allusion as well; for Jessica's nearer eye drew suspiciously toward him, and there was no doubt of the flush on her cheek now.

"If this happy convalescence continues, we shall be able to remove you very soon to more congenial quarters," said her uncle's rich, hopeful voice.

"I have tried worse," replied Chauncey, with a slight shiver. "I mean when I was hung. That was a very bad case of suspended animation, or suspended something. The environment, as Darwin would say, didn't harmonize. But *this* is very pleasant, especially——"

"Hush, you are talking too much," said Jessica, shaking her finger at him in unmerciful interruption. Then turning to her uncle she said, decidedly, "He must not stay here another night."

But Mr. Armstrong had an archaic reverence for medical prerogatives. He replied—

"My dear, in these matters we are at the mercy of the doctors."

"Oh, *I* know," she retorted, wisely.

Chauncey, who was watching her with a placid sense of delight, read in her accent and emphasis—

"I have brought *several* 'doctors' to terms in my day."

"What are you going to do with me?" he asked, presently. "Have you any serious intentions?—as the mouse said to the cat."

"Oh, *we'll* take care of you—Jessica knows," she responded cheerily, with her old-time little bird-like toss of the head.

" Oh, very well, answered he," settling himself comfortably ; " I can stand a good deal of that sort of thing."

Jessica rose quietly and went out of the house. She had caught the sound of approaching wheels, and rightly conjectured that the potentate of whom they had spoken was at hand, for very few vehicles travelled that lonely road-like street. Robert Chauncey could hear by a little effort the low persuasive hum of her voice, now rising into more excited earnestness as if to overcome some obstacle, now dropping into silence with a "dying fall," which suggested a whole battery of arch, sidelong blandishment. He could hear, too, the whimsical astonishment in the male tones of reply; but acquiescence seemed to be gaining upon it, and he knew perfectly well how the battle would go. He could hardly keep his features in respectful trim while the surgeon made his *pro formâ* examination, and uttered his prescribed verdict. He could see then and thereafter that Roger Armstrong's benevolent aspect was tempered with a good deal of shrewd mirth and some little disquietude; but even an extorted official assent, backed by the beloved Jessica's zeal and active will, carried too much weight to be resisted by the older man, while the younger was very willing to accept the risk for the compensation which it brought.

Of course Jessica's affectionate interest in Robert Chauncey was deepened and heightened by the reparation she was making, and the kindnesses which she had done and designed to do. Something curiously like the maternal feeling was developed in her by the certainty that he would be definitely under her wing until his recovery. He smiled whenever he thought of it with a gentle and hopeful sense of amusement; but assuredly neither respected nor loved her the less for this womanly patronage.

His removal was (without explanation) postponed until after dark, in order to avoid the funeral of Charlotte's son, which had been set for that afternoon. In spite of his moral and social eccentricities, "Brother John" had contrived to

II

keep up a sort of intermittently backsliding membership in a populous and frantic negro "society" or congregation, where (when out of the hands of the law) he was held in a sort of uneasy esteem, based upon his professions of grace and the certainty of his vigor.   He had also found it politic to belong to various mysterious organizations for mutual aid and glorifying, which lavished nouns and adjectives on their corporate titles as freely as they decked the persons of their units in all that was cheap and tawdry—quaint and multitudinous outflowerings of the gregarious African nature, exacting little except stylish Sunday clothes and punctilious attendance at meetings during life; and guaranteeing sumptuous obsequies afterwards.   All these now gathered to follow his coffin. Jessica and her uncle on their return were a little startled when they saw the stupendousness of the preparations.

"Zounds and death!" exclaimed Roger, with unwitting relevancy.   "Is this a foreign ambassador whom you have been entertaining unawares?"

"An ambassador from the Prince of Darkness, I reckon," cried his grandson, with a boyish snort of dislike and defiance.

The words impressed Jessica as she stood looking out of a neighboring window.   Then there was a great solemn blare of brass instruments, and the pageant of living ebony stirred. On they moved—the black-faced band of musicians with the massive tubes that shone like gold, the sombre hearse, and the polished blackness of the lines of hired carriages, the black battalion of militia in uniform with sparkling bayonets, and the array of black societies in and out of regalia, with their finery lighted into gorgeousness by the sunset.   The more Jessica gazed after them and listened to the slowly dying music, the more the fancy gained upon her that she had witnessed a procession of evil spirits bearing a lost soul to its doom.   Then, with a sense of its morbidness, she turned abruptly away, wishing that Robert Chauncey were present to occupy her mind with something better and brighter.

If Captain Hawksley had witnessed that funeral, he would have been amused to see his policeman stalking along in resplendent trappings behind the hearse of the slain ruffian who had lately sought his life—not in any romantic stretch of generosity, nor with any sense of incongruity, but simply to render the usual routine honors to an Amalgamated Relative of Moses.

CHAPTER XXII.

"THIS MAD WORLD—GIGMANITY."

During Captain Hawksley's service as an atoner and good Samaritan, his soul, though not without some aches and pangs, had been softened and warmed as by sunshine, and even after he left the spot an aroma of cheerfulness seemed to keep him company. But as his distance increased, this blessing diminished, until he was out in spirit on the darkened waste of commons again.

He entered the cars a moody, lowering man. As the train worked away faster and faster, the trees raced past or wheeled soberly in distant procession, and he seemed to see everything in his life resolving itself into a phantasmal mockery of endeavor. What had come of all his fervent beliefs and strenuous, unsparing efforts? "The sacred political creed of his youth" had gone down under overwhelming force, and even those who had been its partizans were beginning to distrust, if not to deride it. All hopes of restoration now seemed like vapors. He felt that there would be something unfit and portentous in bringing to life a long-buried corpse—a vampire visitant that the world would shrink from and abhor. He did not regret anything that he had done in behalf of that eternally lost cause, nor doubt that it had the very highest sanction. Nor did he arraign the Divine righteousness: he only conceived of it as persistently and unalterably decreeing the very reverse of itself, and bringing confusion on its loyal champions. And withal, the trees hurried by as if to overtake some opportunity, or turned their wheeling into whirling as though suddenly made aware of the exceeding value of time—yet verily stirred not.

In the great downfall much else had gone down; and under the shadow of his present mood his whole career seemed a sad failure. His boyhood's crude aspirations, the maturer resolves of worldly-wise manhood, his vehement endeavors to make himself felt in arms, in politics, in the world of letters— he seemed to stand amid the cold relics and ruins of all. And that dearer ambition of the heart which might have so consoled him for every other loss, which, he had fancied, might indeed, have restored everything—he would not suffer his mind to dwell on it; yet that loss undeniably entered into and darkened every thought. The end of everything would be welcome. He was weary of shows and futilities, of hopes fondly held and duty well done, which yet came to nothing. And now, as though the universe agreed with him, all that was respectable in human institutions were wrestling hope-lessly with the whirlwind and the earthquake. And still the pine pillars sped by, and the weightier oaks of the back-ground circled like dancers in a colossal "hands-all-round"— yet assuredly the morrow's sun would find them in their accustomed places.

While his mind was thus scowling at grievous topics, Cap-ital suddenly made itself audible to him in the salutation—

"Why, friend Hawksley, how is your good health?"

The tone had that sort of surface jollity which one always fancies to have been originally adopted as a good invest-ment, though it may have grown into a habit. There was a comfortableness about it as of a soul just risen from the softest of down, and assured of finding similar provision made for it through life. Its prosperous imperturbability seemed consummate impudence to Hawksley's haughty tem-per. He looked the man over, from his softly-padded cheeks and full person (with a symbolical aggressiveness of gold chains and seals and studs, on a ground of black and white,) to his sleekly-filled pantaloons, newly from the tailor's, and

straddling a little to offset the swaying of the cars.   Then he
looked him over again, up from the unbulging knees and
well-fed abdomen to the hail-fellow-well-met blue eyes, and
answered—

"You have the advantage of me, sir."

"Why, confound it," cried the other, not at all disconcerted,
"don't you remember a certain young devil of a lootenant
that you *didn't* hang in the days of the re——"

"—taliation," put in Hawksley, with something like a sedate
smile.   "Ah! yes—Mr. Coleman, I think?   I did not intend
any discourtesy; but you are not the same kyind of man that
you used to be—in physique I mean."

As he spoke he made room for his ex-enemy, though in
truth such company did not please him.   His dislike for the
"plutocracy" was certainly very different from the hostility of
the strikers; but it was hardly less pronounced.

"I regyarded it as strange, he continued, "that such a
stripling should have a commission."

"Yes?" answered Coleman.   "Well, there was some money
in the family—as you may have happened to hear;" and he
stroked his taut rounded waistcoat with the air of one who
refrains from his lawful privilege of boasting.

Hawksley *did* recollect hearing that this young man's
father had raked so much money out of cinders and refuse,
that now some thousands of men (when not on a strike) were
doing the raking for him, and multitudinous varieties of pick-
ing and hammering as well.   When a base material could be
so readily transformed into a rarer one, or a lower form of
carbon into a higher, the same expeditious process might well
seem applicable to mankind.   But Coleman was not yet a
diamond in Hawksley's eyes; so the latter merely bowed with
a neutral air.

Compelled to take the initiative, Coleman inquired, in a
voice where cordiality struggled against depression—

"Well, how goes it with you, friend Hawksley?   Have you
found the avenoo to riches?   Have you made your pile yet?"

"I have not even made the attempt," answered Hawksley, who was being initiated into active contempt by this refrain of the almighty dollar.

Coleman looked at him as at something incomprehensible.

"Well," said he, with a rather weary prolongation on the last sound. He turned to his newspaper for a moment; but presently looked up again rather excitedly, saying: "Listen to this," and read, "'A general foreboding of continued disasters to life and property occupies the public mind.'"

He laid down the journal, and asked: "What do you think of that?"

"I think 'the public mind' evinces abnormal good sense," replied Hawksley, calmly.

"That's very well for you," said Coleman, with a rueful grimace; "but it's pretty rough noos to a man who has ever so much money at the mercy of the ugliness of those fellows. What is one to do?"

"Fight," answered Hawksley. "Only you diskyarded your best chance fifteen years ago."

"I understand," replied Coleman, after a minute's puzzling; "but I don't agree. However, I hope you will be on the right side this time."

"I fought for the rights of property before, and I am prepared to fight for the rights of property again."

Coleman twisted his face awry with, "There are various kinds of property;" then, summoning his not easily vanquished jollity, he cried: "Come over into Macedonia and help us. I am bound for Philadelphia now. Our regiment is ordered to Pittsburgh to-night. I'll smuggle you in."

"I decline smuggling," answered the captain, wondering as he spoke whether Pittsburgh were not after all the spot where he would be most likely to find Vamper.

"I didn't mean *that*," replied Coleman. "You shall go in with all honors. You will like it, I can assure you—a first-rate set of men. In our regiment there are relations of some of the richest men in Philadelphia."

Hawksley drew away a little, involuntarily, but he answered, "I volunteer." In his heart he was thinking, "Shoulder to shoulder with money-grabbers and abolitionists." But he had never let fastidiousness stand in the way of duty, and he would not now.

In Baltimore they found the air full of the rumors and even the sounds of conflict. At the very time of their brief halt, a disorderly regiment of militia was fighting its way through the lower streets, repulsing charge after charge of a furious mob, and firing volleys in all directions: while bewildered people were dropping here and there in doorways and along the pavement.

On reaching Philadelphia, Coleman and Hawksley promptly repaired to the headquarters of the First Regiment, and the new recruit was gladly accepted in place of a doughty member who had pressing business elsewhere. The expedition set forth without delay, consisting of two regiments of infantry and an artillery company.

On the way to Pittsburgh, Hawksley noticed with a slight deepening of foreboding, that his companions seemed to have a very inadequate conception of the task before them. They were a trim set of young fellows for the most part, drawn largely from the counters and offices of their city, and ready enough to try conclusions (in no spirit of "brotherly love") with the upsetters who menaced their livelihood and comfort; but the prevalent expectation was that there would be just fighting enough to furnish a staple for future anecdotes, leaving them free to return speedily as victors, with a fine crop of laurels and an admiring audience.

About noon of the next day they stepped out of the cars in Pittsburgh, watched by groups of idlers who ventured sly shafts of satire. There was no lack of leisure in the city at that time. The great strike of the railway men had spread to the retainers of nearly every manufacture, and had brought to a standstill the business of many tradesmen and unattached mechanics who depended upon them for support. These were all at liberty to compare grievances on corners and in bar-rooms, and incite one another to measures of resistance and retaliation. There were grimy coal miners, too, and canal men, and behind the rest, waiting their chance, the representatives of a great mass of prowling crime, fostered by public distress, and scenting something not yet to be spoken of.

CHAPTER XXIII.

"TO DEATH UTTERLY."

As the young soldiers looked on the sneering or scowling faces round them their gaiety was moderated, but they had as yet no serious misgiving. There was every readiness to obey, when, about the middle of the afternoon, they were ordered out in support of the sheriff and his *posse*, to clear the railway tracks near the outskirts of the town, which were now occupied and obstructed by a large crowd.

On their appearance, the latter set up a series of derisive calls and cries, steadily refusing to withdraw. Pending the efforts of the civil authorities, the troops were halted on a network of tracks, with the battery a little above them. On each side was rough, open ground, having houses sparsely scattered over it—none very near. In front was a rather steep hillside of yellow clay, washed and gullied by rains, and traversed by ditches, its peculiar hue contrasting in patches with the dark groups which almost covered it. These overflowed from the base, enveloping the flanks of the expedition.

Not all of these people were active rioters. Old men, loiterers, and women, had been led to the spot in numbers ; and not a few children had left their play to gaze at the bright uniforms and partake of the prevailing excitement.

Most of the adults, even, were too ignorant to understand their peril. They could hardly believe that any troops would dare the impiety of firing on the "working men," the "people," the voting sovereigns of the land. Had they not been told year after year, in print and public speech (and especially whenever election time drew near), that they were on an equal footing with kings? And what was it they demanded?—nothing but a fair share in the great division going on about them. True, direful news had come from Baltimore, but that city was far away, and associated with past tales of rebellion and bloodshed; and it rather added to their exasperation and pugnacity, by reminding them that these bayonets and bullets were a threat, however impotent, of terrible evils and suffering. The fact that the threat came from a rival city, which had always overshadowed their own, put compromise almost out of the question.

The sheriff and his men after a brief colloquy were rudely repelled, and the crowd pressed after them almost against the troops, not at all in awe of the weapons; on the contrary, they seemed half minded to take them for toys.

Feeling in a manner straitened, and seeing that matters were growing more serious, the militia were ordered to form a square. The crowd impeded this movement in every way, even jostling the men amid loud hootings, and in some instances striving to wrench their muskets away. Thus far, however, there was an infatuated contempt in the demeanor of the mob, almost amounting to good humor. They were like a gang of boys hauling about a powerful but harmless animal, whose very capabilities to do injury only increase the fun. "You wouldn't stick working men with *them* things? You wouldn't order *working men* about, would you?" were the ironical queries on all sides.

However, this slight collision heated the blood, and the inertness of the young soldiers (who were beginning to look stunned and uncertain) gave their opponents a sense of triumph.

"A foine lot o' doughfaces to come an' boss us," clamored the throng, which was not without its Hibernian elements. Its members were as near as before at every point, leering and jeering into the faces of the men, and jostling forward with spasmodic starts which threatened to end in a general bodily precipitation upon them.

At this juncture the companies facing Yellowside were ordered to advance and clear the space immediately before them. This they did rather nervously, with lowered bayonets, helped by the unchanging composure of Hawksley and one or two other veterans among them. The crowd, taken by surprise, dissolved at that point without even a prick of the steel ; not stopping to argue the question, but rushing away in tumbling groups, which glanced back over their shoulders to see what had so quickly discomfited them. Before they began to reassemble, the troops were back in the square again.

Hawksley had now an opportunity to look around. That feeling of unreality, of being in a dream, which often accompanies rapid shifting of place and surroundings, had been with him ever since he had left Washington; and he had known that the dream would end in a nightmare. He now felt that the nightmare was at hand. There is always something preternatural in human passions of the fiercer and darker sort when aroused in great masses of men and spreading by contagion. You cannot but look for the shadowy whisperer behind the show, who sways them all with the combined power of an elemental force and a sinister will. Hawksley felt this—and watched.

Meanwhile the eastern side of the square had been ordered to advance in its turn. This time there was no surprise. The masses previously dispersed were gathering again, all the more ireful for some twinges of shame, and calling on their comrades not to yield. The latter did give way, nevertheless; but there was a tussle at several points, and one of the militiamen, finding himself overmatched, thrust sharply with his bayonet. He probably had no clear idea of what he was doing, but all the same the blood ran.

From that moment the aspect of the contest changed. There was no more mirth, even of a sarcastic and scornful sort. Before the Grays had returned to their places in the square, stones began falling among them and behind them, and this pelting spread and grew on all sides, accompanied by an uproar of threats, curses, and hideous inarticulated sounds. Here and there disordered figures with wild action pressed through the mob, imparting their real or simulated fury. More than once Hawksley thought he recognized for a moment the face for which he was watching.

The soldier-clerks, stung and smitten by missiles of every size, and half bewildered by the storm of execration round them, were in a state to be carried away by any desperate impulse. First one rifle was discharged; then another. Then Hawksley heard Coleman exclaim excitedly, "Look yonder, he's aiming at us. Not much, by Joshua!" and the report of his piece made the third. Almost simultaneously, a working man, some rods up the slope in front of them, staggered forward with a half-poised shot-gun, which tipped upwards as he fell, discharging both barrels into the air.

The crowd scattered from about him as from a place where lightning had struck; and in the opening thus unexpectedly made, Ishmael Vamper stood plainly revealed. His eye glanced to right and left, as if in search of shelter; then seeing that he must rely on his own arts alone, he began a series of seemingly automatic movements, advancing and receding, swerving and straightening, bowing and rising, leaping and sinking, expanding and contracting, all with such marvellous rapidity, and accompanied by such fantastic leers, grimaces and gestures, as might well have disordered any aim. It is not often that one dances and plays pranks for his life.

Hawksley understood it all, and knew the inevitable result quite as well as Vamper did. There was an assured serenity on his brow as the gunstock flew to his shoulder; and the barrel settling exactly to its level, followed the erratic motions of its living target. The sound of its discharge blended with the command "Fire!" and the fusillade on each side of him. Then the duly authorized ball was sent on a very special and private errand.

At once the expression of mockery flitted from Vamper's face, and something shot into the latter which might have been a shrill, inhuman cry made visible. Every lineament was wrung into appalling shapes, that yet seemed strangely natural. It was more like the dropping of a mask than a transformation. Even the outblaze of an inner hate beyond conception was overcast by the deeper horror of a foreknown and long baffled doom. For a moment his whole frame was stretched and thrilled into abnormal height, both hands beating the air violently backward, as if in an effort to repel. Then he suddenly disappeared, as the fleeing crowd rushed against and over him.

"My God!" cried Coleman. "What a face!"

"He has gone where he came from," said Hawksley, deliberately re-loading.

Coleman glanced at him curiously; then, taking the speech for one of those platitudes which we favor death with, he replied—

"Well, I guess we must all do that. Here goes!" and he fired again.

The militia-men had now passed beyond the control even of themselves, and continued blazing and flashing in all directions—up the tracks, along the cross-streets, over the open lots, into the hillside—in a word, wherever any human being was to be seen—until the absence of targets made them pause.

After the first volley there had been no resistance. It had stricken into the crowd like summer lightning into a throng of cattle. They had scarcely realized what it meant until men began dropping here and there all over Yellowside. The hooting and stone-throwing abruptly ceased. A few tumbled pell-mell into ditches or crouched behind inequalities of the ground; the remainder scrambled away incontinently, impeding and trampling one another, until at last the field was clear. Then the expedition marched back again and took up its station in proximity to the round-house, a strongly-built brick structure with considerable wood-work overhead.

They were beginning to feel already that a tower of refuge
might be needed. So far were they from being elated by their
success that it had cowed them even more than their opponents. They had stayed long enough after the fight to see
their work siripped of all romantic accessories. They had
counted the little children who were writhing and shrieking
with pain or lying very still forever. They had heard the
curses shrieked down to them by mothers reckless with
grief—meanly-clad, kneeling mothers, who tossed wild arms
over their slain sons. They knew that the great aggregate of
public opinion around them would look more to these results
than to their motives or technical authorization. They had
not been long enough segregated from their kind to acquire
the regulars' machine-like assurance of conscience and of
nerve; and in the reflected light of popular reprobation, they
could not but shrink with a guilty and disabled feeling.

CHAPTER XXIV.

"MEN SCARCELY KNOW HOW BEAUTIFUL FIRE IS."

Before long a distant hubbub—gathering, shifting, indeterminate—reached the ears of the militia, and stealthy friends brought them rumors which were scarcely more definite and quite as menacing. They heard that men who were supposed to be their partizans had already been beaten and even killed; that excited mobs were parading various streets with drums and banners; that a general pillaging of gun-shops was in progress; and that the United States armory, as well as the city itself, was in the hands of the rioters. Soon half-armed and very truculent groups began to show themselves in the neighborhood, and the troops were ordered within the round-house. This movement was encouraged by dropping shots from the background, which continued even after they were thus hidden. No harm was done, but one or two bullets came in at the windows and traversed the building in the space above their heads with a most venomous and prophetic sound.

Hawksley and Coleman stood beside one of these openings, peering out cautiously with sombre faces, and listening to the deepening roar.

"Beyond a doubt they have taken the city," said the former, "and now they are coming to pay their regyards to us. What's this in a cyart?"

"They've captured Hutchinson's battery," cried Coleman, in consternation.

"There's only one gun," answered Hawksley, "and wretch-edly mounted.   Something must be broken.   Now, then, look to yourselves."

The last sentence was addressed to an audience out of hear-ing.   As he spoke he sighted deliberately at a man who was trying to get the half-disabled piece into position, and pressed the trigger.   The living target fell, and the gun tumbled partly over him, dragging down one or two more of the riot-ers in its fall.   Before they could extricate themselves, a sharp fire was opened from the windows of the round-house, and another man was killed.   Then the throng about the overthrown cannon scattered for awhile.   Indeed, they never afterward succeeded in making it useful.

By this time the mob was larger than the one dispersed that morning, and infinitely fiercer.   There was a tigerish sound in their yells which made the hearer's blood chill and flutter.   Fresh accessions were continually pouring in from all quarters, exhibiting their spoils and weapons amid shrill cries of welcome.

While the besiegers were thus working themselves into a frenzy, the wagons containing the rations for the besieged came into view.   At once ensued a scene which was a start-ling reminder of the bread riots that preceded the Reign of Terror.   Men in all imaginable, unkempt costumes swarmed over the wagons, gorging themselves like spirits of famine, scattering the fragments broadcast and trampling them in the mire, howling, hooting, dancing—behaving, in short, like most approved French revolutionary demons.   The whole concourse screamed in derision at the sallow-faced crew in the round-house, who would sup on curses only.

"Great heaven! look at that!" exclaimed Coleman.   "And I would give a thousand dollars for something solid to eat!"

"There are *some* things that money cannot compass," replied Hawksley, with slightly satirical sedateness.   "A panther cannot be induced to trade, nor will he accept ransom."

12

" No, I guess not," assented Coleman, ruefully. " I wonder whether these excitable gentry will eat *us*. That *would* be be a consumption of home manufactures. I have always been in favor of protection, but I never wanted it so badly as now."

Hawksley smiled encouragingly at this effort to brew a little jollity and hardihood. Then he said in all seriousness—

" If you escape, and I die, will you be kyind enough to take this kyard to friends in Washington—to the young lady whose address I have penciled there ?"

" Certainly, old fellow," answered Coleman, reaching for the card, and evidently reassured by the chance to show good nature. " But don't talk about dying—it's not cheerful. What's this ? ' Two of your former guests are gone. Good-bye, and may God Almighty bless you and yours forever and ever !' Well, of all the messages to send to a young lady !"

" Will you take it ?" asked Hawksley, frowning.

" Oh, certainly," answered the other, with conciliating alacrity. " It will be a most pleasant dooty. I mean—confound it—I'd give just ten thousand dollars to be out of this place."

Hawksley bowed his thanks, but did not speak. His mind was settling into the solemn mood of one who has done with earthly interests, except the dear friends left behind. " God bless her bright face," thought he, " she will be safe now, and happy ; and she will not utterly forget." Then the last pang of renunciation seized him, and he said to himself, " So be it I have no use for life. It is time to be out of this disjointed world." Then there came into his mind the first words of that impressive early lyric, " Go, soul, the body's guest, upon a thankless errand."

The twilight had now quite died out of the smoky air, and the leaping of bright, distant flames became visible at various points. There was no rush of horses nor clanging of bells, no delirious whirl of engines flung bodily to the rescue. The very boys did not run to look; they had a wilder attraction nearer at hand. Man no longer combated the spirits of destruction; he was their most potent engineer and ally.

The great howling mass of rioters drew nearer than before. Trusting to the darkness, its members hardly sought cover, and the soldiery refrained from firing at random.

On one side of the round-house, the yards of the railway company extended for some distance. Within them were sheds for storing freight and utensils, and trucks which ran up a moderate incline to a sort of platform, where cars were standing row on row, some quite empty, others still densely packed with miscellaneous freight, and not a few containing heaps of bituminous coal or tanks of even more inflammable petroleum. This exposed quarter had been avoided by the mob during daylight; but now a cry of exultation and excitement was heard there, and a shattering of locks and timbers. Presently a flicker of flame rose above one of the more distant buildings; and then another and another. Then the end of a car blazed up and the fire came creeping along it.

At this there were cries of dismay from the huddled, perspiring throng within the round-house; and the dancing glimmer which came through the windows played faintly on ghostly faces and limbs that shook. Under the stress of panic, and hoping that pillage would make a diversion in their favor, the men near the door unbarred it, and three of them sprang out and ran. But they underrated the implacable watchfulness of their enemy. The blood of the children and old men who had fallen on Yellowside was calling more loudly in scores of hearts than any spoils however tempting, or any opportunity for lesser destruction. As soon as the three reached the half-light outside, there was a great shouting of jubilation and execration, and one of them fell dead under a discharge from half a dozen rifles. Then there was a scamper and a struggle, shrieks for mercy blending with pistol shots and heavy blows; and the two other fugitives were lost to man and to life.

Now the firing began again in earnest, for the terror of the militia made them doubly vengeful, and they saw that nothing could be gained by forbearance. The mob fell back a little, but returned the shots from the ground on all sides and from the windows and roof of every neighboring building.

Meanwhile, the scene around the burning cars was terrific. Under the great voluming masses of smoke and shooting yellow flames, a still wilder human saturnalia went on. Men and women, with bare arms, haggard cheeks, and inhuman eyes, frenzied by drink, cupidity, vengeance, and all ungodly excitements, plunged fairly into the fire and dragged out heterogeneous articles of food, apparel, ornament, and household use. Some were struggling with and cursing one another, some hurrying disorderly away to hide their spoils, some dancing in improvised measures as insane and full of menace as the Carmagnole—all howling, hooting, contorting their forms and visages, brandishing newly stolen gleaming arms, brandishing arms that seemed already painted with blood.

As car after car caught fire, the hideous revel drew nearer and stood out from its background in direr vividness, while their motley blades and barrels were in constant coruscation, and their shadows thrown on a wall behind them made a gigantesque multitudinous mocking and mowing, like a silhouette of the infernal regions. Hawksley was tempted to think that he could detect the features of Ishmael Vamper amid these shifting profiles, as though that agitator were the dominant spirit of the scene. Then he smiled to himself at his uncanny fancies, and turned away with a perfect readiness to meet the dead man in this world, or any other, and on any possible terms.

The blaze was now very near and very alarming. Every part of the interior of the round-house could be seen as plainly as in a reddening afternoon sun. The exultant screams and shrieks outside grew wilder and shriller, till it seemed that nothing could possibly be worse. But worse came. In

the climax of the uproar, a flaming box-car was loosened and
started from the upper end of the incline. Down it came
with constantly accelerating speed, until it plunged against
the round-house with a great splintering crash, and flung its
morsels of fire far upward. Some of them were shot through
the windows; and the smoke came pouring after. Before the
first ejaculations of dismay had subsided, a second stroke was
heard that jarred the whole structure, and drops of burning
oil sprayed inside, while the whole outer face of the brick-
work blazed together. Then another car and another and
another came careering down, some laden with oil, some with
coal, others with miscellaneous combustible freight, all plunging viciously into the wreck of their predecessors, and flinging
over everything their blistering showers of solid and liquid fire.
The very walls began to bake and crack under it, and the wood-
work overhead flashed out in several places. The soldiery
were driven from that side of the building and penned together in insupportable heat and mingled glare and darkness.
They could no longer hear the hideous joy of their enemies,
or indeed anything except the crackling and snapping and
roaring close at hand; but now and then a rift in the smoke
to leeward exhibited a tableau which might have been taken
from some dream of torment.

"God in heaven!" exclaimed Coleman, "this seems like the
end of all things."

Under the stress of that Tophet, a sally was now determined
on, with the hope of fighting their way to some refuge. The
arrangements were hastily made, for the blaze was already
spreading over the roof and firebrands dropped upon them as
they stood. When the door opened, their egress was more
sudden than orderly, and the mob, though more or less prepared for it, fell back in all directions. The whole expedition
had reached the open air, and was hurrying with half-formed
ranks towards the suburbs, when their persecutors, recovering,
precipitated themselves on all parts of the column, and most
fiercely on the rear—which included Hawksley and Coleman.

In that sudden howling, half-human surge, the two were separated, and the latter, well buffeted and smarting from a flesh wound, was glad to reach a more solid group of his comrades, who swept him with them to the main body. Looking back from the first enforced halt, he saw Captain Hawksley cut off with one or two others, and forced back to the very doorway of the round-house. Here for a moment there was a pause, while the intense glare behind threw into strong relief his tall, unyielding form and calm, stern visage: then the demoniacal mass of rioters rolled clamorously forward again, bearing him bodily over the threshold, while the jar of their shock against the jambs and wall dislodged a half-burnt beam overhead, which beat him to the ground in its fall, and drove them out beyond the reach of fire.

This was all that Coleman saw, for he was obliged to turn about and take his part in a wretched, desultory struggle of shots exchanged at random and charge and countercharge made without method, which continued until they had traversed the last of the city streets and entered the open country beyond.

It was the last that any one ever saw of Captain Archer Hawksley as a living man: but the next day when his body, less burnt than might have been expected, was removed from the ruins, they found on his face the same inflexible expression which had often marked it. On the fly-leaf of a little Bible in an inside pocket was the signature of Miss Jessica Armstrong, and in his own more recent pencilling the text—"And having done all, to stand."

CHAPTER XXV.

The summer sunshine came cheerily into the room where Robert Chauncey lay comfortably listening to doleful words. These flowed from that fountain of all hopefulness (except in political matters), the genial, ever-youthful Roger Armstrong.

The news had been growing very alarming of late. Three days had gone by since the holocaust in Pittsburgh, and four since the bloodshed in Baltimore, yet the disorders of neither city had been fully quelled; while in a dozen other places (several of them even more important) the insurrection was ablaze. At St. Louis and Chicago, the police, militia, and regulars struggled for life and death against mobs numbering thousands, each collision leaving its *debris* of corpses along the pavements. Far away on the Pacific coast, the respectable elements of San Fracisco, freely armed by the government, were attacking and scattering the tatterdemalion multitudes who gathered to expel the Chinese and rob generally. In Buffalo, a round-house, garrisoned by militia, had been stormed by the rioters. At Reading there had been a slaughter almost equal to that of Baltimore. Fort Wayne and Indianapolis were in possession of the insurgents, and so were all the great lines of communication between the East and the West. New York was preparing for the worst. Even the Cabinet at Washington discussed the proposition to declare several States in revolt, and call out an army of volunteers to restore order.

Nevertheless the sunshine had lost none of its cheery warmth; and Robert Chauncey, with his eyes on Jessica as she sat placidly at her sewing, and his ears less attentive to her uncle's eloquence than to the humming of bees among the honeysuckles outside and the rustling of silvery leaves, could not easily believe that the course of nature would be balked, or that the world was going altogether to the bad. He said very little, except to throw in a pleasant word now and then, which roused the old gentleman from the doze that followed every peroration, and started the symphony again.

"With no power in the hands of capital to compel labor, what *is* to become of these United States? Look at the miserable rahscals, sir, burning and robbing and murdering, with no respect for the rights of property. I have never been an admirer of the mushroom parvenu millionaires of the North; but property is entitled to protection, sir, and anything is more endurable than anarchy. Neither abuse could have existed under our much-abused slavery system, for it fostered standards that were not sordid and habits which prevented inordinate accumulation; while it instilled a respect for vested rights, a deference to social superiors, and a conservative distaste for random innovation, which made even the poorer classes of our people a bulwark of the state—instead of being, as now, its greatest danger. It secured order, sir, and the proper ascendency of intellect; and cultivated a spirit of personal honor which is fast becoming obsolete. The future of this nation, without slavery, seems very dark to me, sir, very dark, indeed!"

Then he dropped his head and dozed comfortably again, while the English sparrows outside, having the field again wholly to themselves, seemed to take up with renewed zest their perennial wrangling, berating, and complaining, as though they, too, were profoundly impressed with one another's mismanagement and the degeneracy of sparrow politics.

Yet Robert Chauncey was disposed to agree with him to a certain point. That is, he felt less critical and revolutionary than formerly. Some old and settled things really seemed as though they might be left without periodical investigation and readjustment; and he could not deny that the present revolt had shown more genius for destruction than regeneration. The only good likely to flow from it was a purely personal one—the advancement of his suit with Jessica.

Lying there with little else to think about, his affection for her had grown and deepened vastly. Down to his leaving Cypress Beach, it had been little more than a flaccid preference, based on congeniality of tastes and certain graces of person and motion, and stung into uncomfortable vitality by her light estimate of himself as compared with Captain Hawksley. Even at the moment of his disaster, there was more of vanity and miscellaneous turmoil in his soul than of anything that promised a durable attachment. But now there was inevitably a certain tie between them, tacitly recognized even by herself; and, moreover, he was made aware that she had grown more settled and balanced in her womanhood, more imbued with the consideration and sympathy which often are born of grievous trouble, more reliably worthy of homage.

He was better able to appreciate such traits since his own very literal plunge into bitter waters. He had been made to see the flimsiness of many things which he had once rated very differently. Even his hitherto dilettante nature stood aghast, and took on a certain retributive sternness as he saw how short a step had all along separated him, with his delicacies and trimmings of body and soul, from the helpless mire of the street and the sewer's foulness. From that time, it often seemed that any suggestion of a return to his old superficial life was positively distasteful. He felt that he had definitely passed a turning point (as happens in more lives than philosophical pessimists like to admit), and was on the road to earnest effort for good. He smiled a little to find that this prospect did not appal him now.

A card was brought up to Jessica.

"Mr. Coleman," she read, with an accent of surprise; then rose tremulously as though with some foreboding.

"I think you had better come, too, uncle," she said, as she passed through the door.

As she entered the parlor, Mr. Coleman rose, a little disturbed by her polite interrogating glance.

"Miss Armstrong?" asked he, hesitatingly.

"Yes, sir," she replied, with anxious courtesy.

"Then here is a card which I was asked to give you by a mutual friend. I was the last person who saw him living."

She took it without a word and carried it to the nearest window, where she stood laboriously reading it through a mist of tears. Just as her uncle entered the room, she broke down utterly and sank into an armchair, covering her face with her hands and quivering mutely.

"What does this mean, sir?" demanded Mr. Armstrong, just entering.

Jessica took on herself the task of explanation.

"He is dead—Captain Hawksley," she said, struggling to speak clearly.

"Zounds and death!" exclaimed her uncle, in consternation. "When? How?"

"It transpired in the great riot at Pittsburgh," answered Coleman.

Then, feeling that this was hardly equal to the occasion, he added—

"Captain Hawksley died like a brave man, doing his dooty."

Jessica rose, saying—

"Mr. Coleman, I am sure you will excuse me. Captain Hawksley was a dear friend of mine."

She passed up to her room and never saw him afterward.

"What does the card mean by two guests being dead?" asked Coleman, with very evident curiosity.

"Was no one else killed that you noticed particularly?" queried Mr. Armstrong, in his turn.

"No," answered the other, reflectively; "unless it might be a sort o' leading spirit among the rioters, a wretched fellow with the most dreadful face I ever *did* see. He was pointing me out for a target—must have known that I represented a great moneyed corporation. I shot his marksman, and Hawksley, alongside of me, shot *him*."

"I suspect you have indicated the man," said Roger Armstrong. "Miserable rahscal! But he is gone elsewhere now, and we will leave him to God's justice—and mercy."

Meantime Jessica was in a state of distracted sorrow. Now that Captain Hawksley was irretrievably lost to her in death, he seemed worthier of admiration than ever before. How very grand he was, going down in that stately Roman way with the wreck of all old systems when he could no longer make head against the new! With what noble steadfastness he had stood to his post in love as in everything else, counting life as nothing when he could no longer hope to win her! And then, oh to think that even in his last hours she owed to him (whom she had driven under the death-cloud) deliverance from a doubt and a terror which would never have wholly left her while Ishmael Vamper lived!

For some days afterward, Robert Chauncey found cause for wonder and pain in her fits of inattention and still more in her over-assiduous efforts to atone. But, after all, living influences are the permanent ones; so there came a time when Captain Hawksley was scarcely more to her than an admired statue in a niche of her memory, and Robert Chauncey was the cheery companion whom she accepted for life.

CHAPTER XXVI.

"REST FROM ALL BITTER THOUGHTS AND THINGS."

Like many another wanderer, this romance returns at the
last to the place of its birth. Once more in the early summer
its people are gathered at Cypress Beach; but this time there
are no shapes nor portents of evil abroad, and perfect sunshine
overflows the whole land. The labor revolt of 1877, with its
sudden terror and its rapid succession of phantasmagoria,
hardly seems to have been at all.

Mrs. Robert Chauncey (our Jessica) is seated, comfortably
sewing, in her rocking chair under the great oak tree where
Vamper received Lieutenant White, assured, graceful, matronly, feeling herself buttressed around by all that gives life
a solid value, and having at easy command those minor luxuries and intangible deferences so dear to delicately nurtured
womanhood. Was there a nightmare long ago and a possi-
bility just missed which might well make one shudder? Best
not to dwell on such unwholesome themes. Perhaps she has
read or dreamed some uncanny fantasy that will not wholly
leave the remoter recesses of her mind, but which assuredly
shall not come out from them to poison her life. For, look
you, this soft grass is certainly very real, and so are the sunshine and the breeze. There is much of magic in the mocking-bird's ecstatic song on the bough above her, but it is a
very good magic; and the little wrens darting in and out of
their holes in yonder dead limb, chitter away in a contented,
housewifely style that warms the heart. The broad fields of
her ancestors stretch away in front and on each side to the

distant woodlands, bathed in light and rich with mellow wheat-billows or glancing sabre-blades of corn. Behind her in the porch she hears the deep, clear, restful voice of her uncle, Roger Armstrong, exchanging old-time pleasantries and didactics with the Hon. Frederick De Lancey, who still occupies his seat in Congress, in defiance of all the Vampers which this or any other world can send forth.

The legislator has just been narrating his interview with Ishmael, and the timely aid rendered by his colored proxy.

" By the Lord, you should have seen him," said he. " He has never recovered from the effects of that exaltation. I believe he thinks himself my *alter ego*, and very nearly as well entitled to a seat in the national councils. He struts so— why there was a very worthy man sent down last session to represent a New England inland district, who came to me with a certain tremulousness of awe upon him, and desired information about that colored *gentleman*."

" Doubtless! doubtless!" laughed Roger Armstrong. " They will all be gentlemen before long. They vote their sentiments already, and soon some one will be discovering that they ought to be installed in the jury box, to pass judgment on the lives and property of our citizens. But they will die out, sir; they must inevitably die out when deprived of the fostering care of the white race, and left to their own improvident devices. It is a pity, too, for the negro is a queer, good-natured creature as any in the world. But as to your Cerberus, he had better luck than Lieutenant White, here, in dealing with that astonishing rahscal."

" Most extrornary behavior !" exclaimed the little man alluded to. " Most extrornary ! I didn't come here that day to qua'l; but I could have shot him as I would a squ'l before I left. But not befo' your do', Miss Jessi—I mean Mrs. Chauncey. Not befo' your do'."

" Thanks !" she answered, smiling demurely.

" Why the fellow had the most brazen assurance," White

went on; "he admitted all sorts of things. Now a gentleman, you know, never admits anything."

" Indeed !" she responded, as though greatly edified.

The lieutenant was a great favorite (rather because of his
little oddities, than in spite of them) at Cypress Beach. He
often rode out from Nodaway, where he was hopefully pursuing the law, and told war stories, which, after the manner
of their kind, grew larger as they grew older. In his case
they derived a unique and rather comical interest from the
fact that he considered himself still in the Confederate service, having somehow contrived to avoid any formal surrender.
Mr. Armstrong used sometimes to laughingly suggest (in his
absence) that perhaps he had been passed over by reason of
his smallness.

Before he had shed any further light on what "a gentleman never" does (whereby so many dogmatists prove trium-
phantly that there *are* no gentlemen), her husband came
briskly up the drive on horseback. Robert Chauncey was
a trifle sturdier of frame, browner of face, and more springy
and positive of tread than formerly, as though he and life had
clasped hands with earnest heart; and this appearance of
change was not misleading. He had developed a talent and
taste for practical farming and the management of affairs,
which would at one time have seemed to him quite in-
credible. A considerable part of the Cypress Beach estate
was under his supervision, beside some little property of his
own, the first payments on which had been made by his
earnings in a very different field. The idle days and long
evenings of midwinter had given him ample opportunities to
ply his brush and palette, and he had done some work of
original quality, in which local influences might be traced.
Some of his productions had traveled to far cities, and won
notice there. Of these, perhaps the most striking was " The
Lady of the Ring"—you could hardly tell whether a spectre
or a living figure, so enwrapped was she in cypress glooms,
sand gleams, vapors, and dim moonlight—so wildly lighted

in eye and form by the swell and strain of an inner agony, that she seemed the very embodiment of pangs and terrors which would surely outlive life.

Another, more cheerful if less ambitious, shows a quadroon girl, meagrely clad, but of well-rounded, creamy beauty, who has stepped into the sunshine, between two low-hanging cypress boughs, holding lightly with both upraised hands the sides of a bucket of water which is poised upon her head, while, seemingly forgetful of her burden, she gazes with indolent curiosity, presumably at a passing boat. A spring below her bare feet overflows from a sunken barrel which is broken away at the front.

Both the artist-farmer and his wife were great favorites with all classes of the community by reason of their sunny, social traits and readiness to be helpful in time of need. The fact of Jessica's temporary disappearance some years before had become almost as misty to the public mind as to that of her uncle himself. It was not easy for gossip to persist in ill-natured suggestions, when the object of them was so conspicuously kind and cordial, and showed such an imperturbable and unconscious front. Gradually the idea spread that the real companion of her elopement was the young man whom she married not very long afterward, and that it would be most wisely treated as a youthful escapade having no further significance.

As Robert dismounted at the edge of the circle in which the drive terminated, his wife came lovingly forward to meet him; while simultaneously their little Ellen and Alice left off chasing grasshoppers, and ran toward him up the gentle slope with breathless laughter and much shaking of arms and bodies and twinkling of feet. Alice, though the younger, was first on the ground. Indeed, she was first in most things, for Ellen's movements, both mental and physical, were often amusingly deliberate and weighty. A very wise, healthful child was little Nell; ready enough to ramble and scamper and make dandelion chains with all earnestness, when not too much engrossed in scrutinizing the problems of the universe.

" I've just come from the Quaker meeting-house over the river," said our reformed communist. "They've had very queer times around there—any amount of scandal among our drab-cloth friends! Oddly enough the—heroine—of it tells a rediculous, superstitious story about a ring which she claims to have found long ago, and which must be very like the one that you lost about the time of my first visit to Cypress Beach. Don't you remember, my dear?"

" I do," she answered in a low, uncomfortable voice.

" Well, she lays the whole blame on that ring in the most absurd way. I thought it might be yours, and tried to get sight of it; but her father had flung it into the Pocomoke."

Jessica replied, with an air of relief—

" It was best. I don't wish to see the thing again."

Robert stared; for she had never brought herself to be quite frank with him on the subject. Indeed that was hardly possible, since she lacked words to define some of her bygone fancies about Vamper and that strange gem. They seemed almost like touches of insanity; and what had actually occurred was really by comparison so little!

His brow began to cloud, but before he spoke the sage Ellen made a diversion. After her usual fashion, she had brought a topic with her, and pursued that train of thought, disregarding all else.

" Papa," said she, "you told us the other day about a man who made a bargain with the great debil" (here her voice sank into a confidential whisper and her eyes grew larger) " not to say his prayers, if the debil would let him fly like a bird. An' he forgotten an' said his prayers one day, an' the debil falled him in the water. Was that bad in the man? or was it bad in the debil?"

" It was bad in both of them," answered the mother for him.

But Ellen was not at the end of her ethics.

"Was it bad in the man to promise the debil not to say his prayers? or was it bad in him to say his prayers after he had promised the debil not to say 'em?"

"Now, Jessica," exclaimed her husband, with somewhat of expectant triumph. But she was equal to the occasion.

"It was wrong to make such a promise," she said.

"Well done, diplomatist!" cried Robert.

Ellen turned to him again with her next.

"Did you ever know that man, papa?"

"I knew a man who had something like that happen to him. It was no good thing."

Here little Alice made her contribution, speaking with mincing preciseness:

"I think that man must have been mor-tee-fied when he found he had tumbled into a mudpuddle."

"Now, you bet you; I should say so!" exclaimed her father, laughing and patting her sunny head. "Run off and fetch me some 'hoppers."

At this up came Mammy Charlotte, a little more rheumatic than formerly, but otherwise unchanged.

"Good mornin', Mr. Robert," said she; "Miss Jessie, I've been a runnin' an' a sarchin' till my ole bones ache like dey would split; an' whar is de consecrated lye?"

"We had it here a moment ago," answered Chauncey. "I gave it to the children yesterday."

Charlotte looked after them, evidently puzzled.

"Laws, Miss Jessie!" said she, "how dey does favor you—specially de light complected one, little Miss Alice! But what shell I do about de consecrated lye?"

Here Prince (now developed into an awkward but very popular stripling just home for the holidays) looked up from the novel that he was reading in a good grassy, sprawling place, and said—"You had better go to a minister for that sort of thing, Mammy."

The fact is he was beginning to catch a little of the iconoclastic spirit of the time, and felt that he had already learned

13

enough at school to be astutely critical in legendary and
sacerdotal matters. So it gave him pleasure to second his
cousin-in-law in this way.

But the patriarch of their little household had caught their
words, and felt called upon to put in a protest.

"Now that's hardly fair," said he. We ought always to be
deferential to gentlemen of sacred character. When I was a
youngster, I knew one of them who used to ride up on horseback, to rap on the parlor windows, and call, 'Any communi-
cants for to-morrow!' And I have heard that once when the
hounds came by he was so transported, sir, that he sprang to
his saddle and put off after them in his surplice. He often
used to escort young ladies to their carriages after service,
without stopping to make a change of raiment. Yet he was
always treated with the most distinguished consideration."

Turning to Mr. De Lancey, he added—

"Those were rare old times, sir."

"They were indeed, sir," responded the Honorable Frederick ; and the two gentlemen of an elder era shook their heads
in company in a whimsical, traditional regret that was at least
half conscious of its own absurdity.

Thus life flows on for Jessica, brightening with every year
and clearing itself of all shadows, pleasantly broken now and
then by a return to more artificial enjoyments, but for the
most part with a current as equable and genial as the lapse of
one summer dream into another.

THE END.

www.ingramcontent.com/pod-product-compliance
Lightning Source LLC
Chambersburg PA
CBHW022351020726
47500CB00002B/226